BLOSSOM FORD MOMS

THE ENTIRE COLLECTION

IRIS WEST

Blossom Ford Moms

Copyright 2025 Iris West

All rights reserved.

This is a work of fiction. Any references to historical events, real people, or real places are used fictitiously. Other names, characters, places and events are products of the author's imagination, and any resemblance to actual events or persons living or dead is entirely coincidental.

No part of this book may be reproduced in any form or by any electronic or mechanical means, including information storage and retrieval systems, without permission in writing from the author. The only exception is by a reviewer, who can quote a short excerpt in a review.

FREE BOOK

Would you like a free book? Sign up to my mailing list at https://dl.bookfunnel.com/t191w45ryj to receive a copy of Loving My Fake Husband, a Curvy Brides of Blossom Ford Series short story.

SINGLE MOM AND THE MOUNTAIN MAN

BLOSSOM FORD MOMS BOOK 1

IRIS WEST

Chapter 1
SIENNA

WHY DID I EVER think I needed a man to be truly happy?

The question flits through my mind as I take in a deep breath of fresh mountain air, the scent of pine and wildflowers filling my lungs. It's a hot, sunny Friday afternoon in May, but up here in the mountains, there's a cool breeze that makes it perfect for camping. My six-year-old daughter, Bree, skips ahead of me on the narrow trail, her backpack bouncing with each step, and a surge of love so strong it almost takes my breath away, washes over me.

"Mommy, look at that butterfly!" She exclaims, pointing to an azure butterfly fluttering past us, eyes wide with wonder.

"It's beautiful, sweetie." My heart swells. This is happiness. It's all I need. This, the friendship of the three single moms who've become like sisters to me, and this town that welcomed me when I came here six years ago, pregnant and broken-hearted, my dreams shattered. Without the man I thought was the love of my life, I figured my life was over. I don't think that way anymore.

Growing up, my nose was perpetually stuck in a book. My parents, both busy academics, left me largely to my own devices, and I coped with the loneliness by dreaming of having a loving family of my own someday, like the characters in the book. I wanted it all–the meet-cute, the whirlwind romance, the happily ever after.

"Can we rest for a bit?" Bree's voice pulls me from my thoughts. "My feet are tired."

I guide her to a fallen log just off the trail. As we sit, I pull out our water bottles and some trail mix. "Here you go, sweetie. A little snack to keep us going."

As Bree munches happily on the mix of nuts and dried fruit, I gaze at the mountains in the distance, their peaks still capped with snow despite the warmth of the day. Wildflowers dot the meadow nearby, splashes of purple, yellow, and white against the lush green grass.

It's peaceful and what I need after finishing three back-to-back projects.

"Mommy? Can we keep going now? I want to find the perfect spot for our tent!"

I ruffle her hair. "Let's go find that perfect place."

As we continue our hike, Bree chatters excitedly about all the things she wants to do this weekend. Her enthusiasm is infectious, and I get caught up in her excitement.

"Let's put the tent here, Mommy."

We've stumbled upon a small clearing surrounded by tall pine trees. The ground is flat, there's a nearby stream and a natural windbreak provided by a cluster of large boulders.

It's perfect–secluded enough to feel like we're in nature, but not too far from the main trail. "This is great. Let's unpack."

We've been to camping sites before, but this is our first time venturing out into the woods alone. I researched the area thoroughly, ensuring it was safe for camping. There's something thrilling about being out here, just the two of us, ready to face whatever nature throws our way.

"Can I help put up the tent?" Bree asks, eyes shining with eagerness.

"Of course, sweetie. Why don't you start by laying out the groundsheet while I sort out the poles?"

As we work together, chattering excitedly about our plans for the weekend, I feel a sense of pride wash over me. We make a great team, Bree and I. Who needs a man when you have a daughter who's your best friend and adventure buddy rolled into one?

But even as I think about it, a small part of me aches. It's the part that still remembers what it felt like to be held, to be kissed, to be loved. The part that sometimes wakes me up in the middle of the night, longing for a warm body next to mine.

I shake my head, trying to dispel these thoughts. I made a choice; I remind myself. After Bree's father bailed, I focused on my child and career. And I'm happy, aren't I?

"I did it!" Bree's voice breaks into my thoughts, and I turn to see her beaming at me, the groundsheet perfectly laid out.

"Great job, sweetie!" I push my conflicting emotions aside. This weekend is about Bree and me, about making memories, about spending quality time together.

I'm so caught up in our tent-building and my own swirling thoughts I don't notice the small rock in my path. My foot catches on it, and before I know it, I'm tumbling to the ground.

I cry out as pain shoots through my right ankle.

"Mommy!" Bree rushes to my side, her face a mask of worry. "Are you okay?"

I try to stand, but the moment I put weight on my right foot, pain lances up my leg. "I think I've hurt my ankle, sweetie," I keep my voice calm for Bree's sake.

Bree's lower lip trembles.

I take a deep breath, pushing down the frustration bubbling up inside me. This isn't how our perfect camping trip was supposed to go. "It's okay, honey. We just need to think this through."

I try to stand again, gritting my teeth against the pain. Mind over matter, right? But after a few failed attempts, I admit defeat. We need help.

I rack my brain for options. My friends will come if I call. It's just that Destiny must be exhausted after a long week at work and picking up her toddler from daycare. Scarlett's probably getting ready for her night shift at the hospital, and Rosa's likely worn out from a day of baking. It will also become dark soon, and none of them know these mountains well. It'll have to be nine-one-one.

"Sweetie, can you pass me my phone? I'm going to call for help."

Bree retrieves my phone from my backpack, and I quickly realize we have another problem – no signal. Great. Just great.

I look around, assessing our situation. We're not too far from the main trail, but the thought of sending Bree to look for help alone in this unfamiliar part of the mountain makes my stomach churn.

"Bree, come here." I open my arms. She snuggles into me, her small body trembling. "It's going to be okay. We'll be okay, alright?"

She nods against my chest.

As I consider our next move, a bark echoes through the trees. Bree's head snaps up, her eyes wide with curiosity. A moment later, a black and white dog comes bounding towards us, its tail wagging furiously.

"Look, Mommy!" Bree exclaims, her earlier fear forgotten in the face of this new excitement.

The dog approaches us, and Bree cautiously holds out her hand. It sniffs her fingers gently, its tail still wagging.

"Be careful," I warn, but I can't help but smile at the joy on Bree's face as she pets the friendly dog.

The dog lets out another loud bark, and this time, I hear a deep voice calling out, "Spot! Where are you, boy?"

My heart skips a beat as a tall figure emerges from the trees. As he gets closer, I stare, momentarily forgetting about the pain in my ankle.

He's easily over six feet tall, in his thirties, with straight brown hair that sits on top of his massive shoulders and a beard I want to sink my fingers into. But it's his eyes I'm most drawn to–a deep, mesmerizing blue that seems to look right through me. He's handsome in a rugged way that makes my pulse race.

Concern etched on his face; he jogs the last few steps to us.

"Are you okay?" His deep voice sends a shiver down my spine.

I open my mouth to respond, but for a moment, no words come out. Get it together, Sienna! "I, uh, I think I've sprained my ankle," I say.

He crouches next to me, and I catch a whiff of his scent–a mix of pine and something uniquely masculine. "I'm Romeo," he says with a small smile. "Mind if I look?"

Romeo. Of course, he would have a name like that. "I'm Sienna and this is my daughter, Bree."

He examines my ankle, asking questions about where it hurts and how it happened. His large hands are deft and surprisingly gentle.

"Looks like a bad sprain. You'll need to stay off it for a few days."

Disappointment washes over me. "So much for our camping trip."

Romeo's eyes meet mine, and for a moment, I forget how to breathe.

"My cabin's near here. I have a portable x-ray machine there. We can check to ensure nothing's broken, and you two could rest up."

I hesitate, glancing at Bree, who's still happily petting the dog. Can I trust this stranger, no matter how kind he seems?

As if sensing my uncertainty, Romeo adds, "I'm a trained medic. I promise you and Bree will be safe."

There's something in his eyes, a sincerity that makes me want to believe him. Plus, the thought of Bree having to spend the night out here with me injured makes the decision easier.

"Thank you."

Romeo turns to Bree and smiles. "I'm going to take you and your mom to my house, so I can treat her ankle, okay?"

She stares at him, her brown eyes, so much like mine, assessing. She nods, then carries on petting Spot.

Quickly and quietly, Romeo packs the groundsheet and tent poles into my backpack and secures the bag on his chest. Then he crouches in front of me with his broad back to me.

"Can you get on my back?"

I bite my lip. I'm about to put my body flush against a man's. It's been ages since I've done that.

I place my arms around Romeo's neck and ease onto his back. He holds onto my thighs and stands like I weigh nothing.

As I feel the solid strength of his arms around me, smell the intoxicating scent of his skin, I'm hit with a realization that both thrills and terrifies me: after years of being indifferent to men, I've found one that makes my pulse race.

Chapter 2
ROMEO

SIENNA FEELS RIGHT WITH her arms, body and thighs wrapped around me, like she was made to be there. Her scent of cherries fills my nostrils as I piggyback her towards my cabin, Bree skipping ahead with Spot.

As we make our way along the familiar path to my cabin, I'm acutely aware of every point where our bodies touch. The softness of her caramel fudge skin, the warmth of her breath against my neck, the way her arm instinctively tightens around my shoulders when we navigate an uneven stretch of ground is intoxicating. I find myself both craving more and wanting to put distance between us.

With her wealth of black curls, oval face, curves that make my mouth go dry and expressive, rich brown eyes, she is the most beautiful woman I've ever seen

"Do you rescue many people up here?" She asks, breaking the silence that had fallen between us.

"Not as many as you might think." I step over a fallen log. "Most people don't camp around here–a lot of the land is private property."

"Oh."

I can almost hear the gears turning in her head. Her brows are probably furrowed, like they were when I suggested she and Bree go to my cabin.

"Well, I know a few people who live close by," she says.

I suppress a chuckle. She's trying to let me know she's not completely alone up here, that there are people she could call on if I turned out to be a threat. It's smart of her, but I'm familiar with every cabin and its occupants in these mountains. If I were a bad guy, she wouldn't stand a chance.

But I'm not a bad guy. Wanting to kiss her cherry lips and taste every inch of her skins feels so good, it can't be bad.

"So, why do you have a portable x-ray machine?"

"It's not actually mine," I explain, carefully picking my way around a cluster of rocks. "I run a security company with some friends. The x-ray machine belongs to the company."

"Are you a salesman or something?"

I laugh, the sound echoing through the trees. "Do I not look like one?"

She's quiet for a moment, then her voice breathless, she says, "Not with those arms. You look more like a soldier."

The memories of my time in the service flash through my mind — the camaraderie, the adrenaline, the pain. I push them away, focusing instead on the present, on the warm weight of Sienna on my back.

"Ex-soldier. I'm a security expert now. The company I work for provides security systems and personal protection services. Sometimes our clients get hurt, and it's convenient to have an x-ray machine on hand." Especially when we rescue vulnerable people on the run from a family member.

"Like a bodyguard? Doesn't Rory O'Connor do something like that? He also lives around here."

I'm not surprised by her words. The O'Connors contribute a lot to Blossom Ford. It would be hard to find anyone in town who hasn't heard of them. Also, Rory was an elite international MMA fighter. It's no secret his security firm protects some of the world's well-known public figures.

"We work together. I take care of admin."

My place comes into view. It's a log cabin with a clear space out front and is surrounded by trees on three sides. My truck is parked in front. I built the cabin with my own hands, a testament to my determination to overcome the limitations others tried to place on me after my injury.

"It's beautiful!" Sienna exclaims.

Pride swells in my chest at her words. "Thanks." I try to keep my voice neutral. "It's home."

Bree stares at us from the porch. She's so tiny, I want to protect her. Spot must feel the same way because he hasn't wandered from her side.

I carry Sienna inside, gently set her down on the sofa and take the x-ray machine out of a kitchen cupboard.

"Any chance you might be pregnant?"

The thought of another man touching her makes my insides boil. I force a smile as I wait for her answer.

"No, definitely not pregnant." There's a pink tinge to her caramel skin.

While I set up the machine, I watch out of the corner of my eye as Sienna takes in the living space. Her gaze roams over the rustic furniture, the stone fireplace, the bookshelves lining one wall. But it's the lone picture on the mantle that captures her attention; a group shot of me with the security team, Rory's wife Bonnie, Rory's parents and aunt outside Rory's cabin.

"I met Bonnie at the O'Connors' annual St. Patrick's Day celebration a couple months back and watched her perform," she says, her eyes lighting up with recognition. "I love her voice and songs, but could never afford her concerts."

"Bonnie's great," I agree.

Sienna sits back, as if the fact that I know the O'Connors helped her decide I'm safe.

While I'm positioning the x-ray machine, Sienna winces when she moves her foot. A protective instinct surges through me, surprising in its intensity. I want to take away her pain, make everything better. It's a feeling I'm not used to, and it unnerves me.

"This might be uncomfortable," I warn her as I steer her ankle to get the right angle. "Let me know if it hurts too much."

She bites her lower lip. The sight sends a jolt of heat through me, and I have to force myself to focus.

After I take the x-rays and confirm it's just a sprain, Bree comes bounding into the room, Spot at her heels. "Mommy, can we stay here tonight? Please? Spot wants to play some more!"

"You know," I hear myself saying before I can think better of it, "If you and Bree still want to spend some time in the mountains, you're welcome to use my spare bedroom. You can spend the day by the pond tomorrow."

Bree's eyes light up at the suggestion.

"We can't impose like that," Sienna says, her eyes darting between me and Bree. "Mrs. Butler might not like it."

"There is no Mrs. Butler." I'm surprised by how important it suddenly seems that she knows I'm single. "Unless you have someone waiting for you at home, you're welcome to stay."

The moment the words leave my mouth, I want to take them back. What am I doing? I've spent years keeping people at arm's length, protecting myself from the pain of rejection, of disappointment. And now, in the span of a few minutes, I'm inviting a virtual stranger and her daughter to stay in my home?

But as I gaze at the mix of hope and hesitation in Sienna's eyes, I can't bring myself to rescind the offer. There's something about her that makes me want to be close to her, to protect her and Bree.

"Nobody is waiting at home. It's just Mommy and me. We have the entire weekend to camp." Her soft brown eyes are huge on her small face.

As I wait for her answer, I realize I'm holding my breath. It's ridiculous, really, how much I want Sienna and Bree to stay in the house I built.

It's a dangerous feeling. I should keep my distance. The thought of potentially seeing disgust or pity in Sienna's beautiful eyes at the sight of my prosthetic legs, covered by my long jeans, makes my stomach churn. Watching a woman flee in disgust after seeing my stumps is an experience I don't wish to repeat.

But as Sienna's eyes meet mine, soft and considering, I hope she'll take a chance on me. Because for the first time in a long time, I'm feeling something other than the weight of my past and my disability. It's the hope that maybe, just for a weekend, I can pretend to have a family and enjoy the warmth and comfort a family shares.

"I suppose it would be a shame to waste a perfectly good camping weekend," she finally says.

As Bree cheers and Spot barks excitedly, a grin spreads across my face. It's just a weekend, I tell myself. What could happen in two days?

But deep down, as I watch Sienna's eyes crinkle with laughter, I know I'm in trouble. Because something tells me, one weekend might not be enough.

Chapter 3

SIENNA

I SETTLE ONTO THE plush couch in Romeo's living room, carefully propping my injured ankle on a pillow. The ice pack Romeo wrapped around it is blessedly cool against my swollen skin. I watch as Romeo moves about the open-plan kitchen, his movements efficient and purposeful as he gathers ingredients from various cupboards and the refrigerator.

"I hope you two like pizza," Romeo calls over his shoulder. "I was planning to make some for dinner tonight."

Bree's eyes light up. "Can I help?" she asks eagerly, bouncing on her toes.

Romeo glances at me, a question in his eyes.

"Go ahead, sweetie. Just be careful and listen to Mr. Romeo, okay?"

"It's just Romeo." He winks, and my heart skips a beat.

Romeo turns to Bree, his expression softening. "Alright, little chef, let's wash our hands."

IRIS WEST

I watch as Romeo patiently helps Bree wash her hands, even providing a step stool so she can reach the sink comfortably. The domesticity of the scene makes my heart ache with a longing I thought I'd buried long ago. This is what I had always wanted for Bree - a father figure to guide her, to share in these everyday moments that seem so small but mean so much.

"Now we need aprons," Romeo announces. He reaches into a drawer and pulls out two aprons. He helps Bree put on the one adorned with colorful fruits and vegetables. The second one, which he dons himself, makes me burst out laughing.

"Is that... Cookie Monster? I didn't peg you for a Sesame Street fan."

"It is Cookie Monster." Bree points to Romeo's chest, eyes wide.

Romeo looks down at his apron, a slight blush coloring his cheeks. The bright blue fabric is emblazoned with a large image of one of my favorite Sesame Street characters, complete with googly eyes and a half-eaten cookie.

"Rory's mom made it," he explains, a sheepish grin on his face. "She has this thing about making sure we all eat properly, so she thought this would be a funny reminder."

"It's adorable," I say.

As Romeo and Bree work on the pizza dough, I find myself captivated by their interactions. He is patient and attentive, explaining each step to Bree so she can understand. He shows her how to measure the flour, guiding her small hands as she pours it into the bowl.

"Now comes the fun part," Romeo says, his eyes twinkling. "We get to mix it all together with our hands!"

Bree's eyes widen with excitement. "Really? We can use our hands?"

"It's the best way to make sure everything is mixed properly. And, it's fun!"

Bree plunges her hands into the bowl, giggling as the flour and water squish between her fingers. Romeo joins in, his large hands probably dwarfing Bree's as they work the dough together.

"Let's get all the flour mixed in," Romeo says gently. "We don't want any dry spots."

As they work, a small cloud of flour puffs up, leaving a dusting of white on Bree's nose. I stifle a laugh, not wanting to interrupt the moment.

"You've got a little something on your nose, munchkin," Romeo says, tapping his own nose to show where.

Bree goes cross-eyed, trying to see her nose, which only serves to spread the flour further across her face. Romeo chuckles, reaches for a kitchen towel.

He wipes the flour from my little girl's face. He's so gentle with her, so caring, that my heart constricts.

"Thanks, Romeo!" Bree chirps, beaming up at him. "Can we make the sauce now?"

"Not just yet. We need to let the dough rest for a bit. We can prepare the toppings. What's your favorite pizza topping?"

"Pepperoni! With lots of cheese!"

Rome's lips curve up.

"Me too. Pepperoni and cheese it is. How about you, Sienna?"

I'm so lost in thought, I startle when I hear my name.

"I like vegetables on my pizza. Maybe some bell peppers and onions?"

"Veggies it is. Bree, want to help me chop some peppers?"

I tense slightly, my maternal instincts kicking in at the thought of my six-year-old handling a knife.

"Don't worry," Romeo says. "I have a special kid-safe knife that can cut vegetables but not little fingers. It's what we use when I volunteer at the community center's cooking classes for kids."

"You volunteer to teach kids cooking?"

Romeo shrugs.

"I filled in once Rory's aunt. After that, I figured they could use more male volunteers."

As Romeo sets Bree up with the kid-safe knife and some bell peppers, I reevaluate my initial impressions of him. This mountain of a man, with his rugged exterior and apparent solitary lifestyle, has layers I hadn't expected. The way he interacts with Bree, his volunteer work with children - it all paints a picture of a man with a genuinely kind heart.

"How's your ankle?"

"Better, thanks. The ice is helping."

"I'll replace the ice soon."

The concern in his eyes makes me feel cared for. I settle back into the couch, and watch Bree focus on her pepper-chopping duties, her little tongue poking out in concentration, and Romeo move between the counter and the stove, where a pot of tomato sauce is now simmering.

The aroma of herbs and garlic fills the air, making my stomach rumble. I can't remember the last time I had a home-cooked meal that I hadn't prepared myself. The thought makes me a little sad. As much as I love my life with Bree, sometimes the weight of single parenthood feels overwhelming.

"Mommy, look!" Bree's excited voice pulls me from my thoughts. "I chopped all the peppers!"

"That's wonderful, sweetie. You're being such a big help."

"Maybe we've got a future chef on our hands."

Bree beams at the compliment, her chest puffing out with pride. "Can I help with the sauce too?"

"Of course. I'll show you how to stir it so it doesn't stick to the bottom of the pot."

As Romeo lifts Bree up so she can reach the stove safely, a lump forms in my throat. My daughter should have moments like this. It's bittersweet to watch, knowing that this is just a temporary moment, a fleeting glimpse into what could have been.

"I think the dough has rested enough. Ready to shape our pizzas?"

Bree practically bounces with excitement.

"You okay?" Romeo asks, gaze intent on me.

I shake my head, forcing a smile. "Just enjoying watching you two work your culinary magic."

I can tell he isn't fooled, but he turns back to Bree. "Okay, little chef, we're going to divide the dough into two pieces - one for each pizza."

I watch as Romeo guides Bree through the process of shaping the pizza dough.

"Now for the fun part," Romeo says, a mischievous glint in his eye. "We get to toss the dough!"

"Really?" Bree's eyes are wide.

"Really. But we have to be careful. Watch me first."

I hold my breath as Romeo demonstrates, tossing the dough into the air with a practiced flick of his wrists. It spins gracefully before landing back in his hands, slightly larger and thinner than before.

"Wow!" Bree exclaims. "Can I try?"

"Let's do it together the first time."

He stands behind Bree, his large hands guiding her smaller ones as they toss the dough together. I can't help but laugh at the look of sheer joy on my daughter's face as the dough flies into the air.

"We did it!" Bree shouts, as the dough lands safely back in their hands.

As they spread sauce and sprinkle cheese and toppings onto the pizzas, I wish I could join in. It's been so long since I've done something as simple as making pizza from scratch. Between work and taking care of Bree, convenience foods have become more the norm than I like to admit.

Bree giggles as Romeo slides the pizzas into the oven. "Did you see, Mommy? I made pizza!"

"I saw, sweetie. Great job."

As I watch Romeo and Bree tidy up and set the table, the fragrant aroma of baking pizza fills the air. I realize I want this to be a part of our lives. I want to laugh with Romeo and Bree as we cook together and mess up in the kitchen.

Chapter 4

ROMEO

THE CABIN IS QUIET. I sit on the porch swing, an ice-cold beer in my hand. The night air is crisp and carries the scent of pine and wildflowers. I inhale, letting the peaceful silence of the mountains wash over me.

Insomnia is an old friend. After years in the army, nights of fitful sleep punctuated by hypervigilance have become the norm. Even here, in the relative safety of my mountain refuge, it's hard to rest. Tonight, it'll take me longer to fall asleep. I can't stop thinking about the warmth of Bree's laughter, Sienna's rich brown eyes and the way her curvy body felt against mine.

The cabin door opens. I turn to see Sienna stepping onto the porch, her hair slightly mussed from sleep, wearing an oversized sweater over her pajamas. The moonlight casts a soft glow on her face, highlighting the gentle curves of her cheeks and the warmth in her eyes.

"Can't sleep?" I ask, my voice barely above a whisper in the quiet night.

She shakes her head, a rueful smile playing on her lips. "No, I just... I needed some fresh air. Do you mind if I join you?"

I point to the space beside me. She uses the crutches I gave her to maneuver herself onto the seat.

"Beer?"

"Sounds great, thanks." She tucks a stray strand of hair behind her ear.

I retrieve another beer from the cooler by my feet and hand it to her. For a moment, we sit in comfortable silence, the only sound the gentle creaking of the swing and the chirping of crickets in the distance. I'm acutely aware of Sienna's presence beside me, the subtle scent of her shampoo mingling with the mountain air.

"It's beautiful out here." Sienna scans the star-filled sky. "So peaceful. I don't think I've ever seen so many stars."

I sip my beer. "That's why I love it up here. The city has its charms, but there's something about the mountains that just... centers you, you know?"

Sienna turns to me, curiosity in her eyes. "Don't you ever find it lonely, though? Being so isolated?"

I think about her question. "I grew up in New York City, so sometimes it is. But after my time in the army, the silence and tranquility is comforting. It helps quiet the noise in my head."

Talking about my past isn't easy, yet I want her to know something about me.

"It must be a big change from military life."

"I loved serving my country. My mom passed when I was little. I had so many step moms, I stopped caring. Being in the army was like finding a family. The camaraderie, the sense of purpose, was great. It lasted twelve years. Then I was severely injured in an explosion and was discharged."

I gulp the beer down, letting the iced liquid burn my throat, as the familiar guilt of being the only survivor of my team sours my mouth.

"Up here, I can breathe. What about you? Have you always lived in Blossom Ford?"

Under the porch light, I make out Sienna's furrowed brows. She hesitates, as if figuring out whether to ask questions. Then she tilts her beer bottle and drinks. I watch the elegant slope of her throat and get distracted by the exposed, tantalizing skin.

"I'm from Garnet City. My parents and I used to spend a couple of weeks of summer break here, now and then. They'd spend the entire time preparing to teach the new semester and let me wander around. I fell in love with the town. When I fell pregnant with a fellow sophomore in college, I was devastated he didn't want the baby. My parents agreed I should abort."

I can't understand how any man would give up the chance to make a family with Sienna. No matter the circumstances.

"That must have been hard."

Sienna lets out a soft, humorless laugh. "They are both professors and love academia. They didn't plan on having me. By the time Mom found out she was pregnant, it was too late to abort. They nurtured me to follow in their paths and I thought I was happy with that. Being a mom changed everything. I moved here a few months before Bree was born, hoping to start afresh."

My heart aches for the teenager she was, pregnant and alone, trying to provide a good life for her baby. Admiration for the strength it must have taken to go against her parents' wishes surges in me.

"You were very brave."

"In the beginning, there were days I feared I'd return home and do what they wanted, but later, I realized that leaving, making my way, was freeing. Don't get me wrong, being a single mom is the hardest thing I've ever done. There are days when I'm so exhausted I can barely think straight. But Bree... she's worth every struggle, every sleepless night."

I'm struck by the strength and determination in her voice. The moonlight catches a glint of unshed tears in her eyes. Resisting the urge to reach out and comfort her takes everything in me. "You're an amazing mom, Sienna. Bree's lucky to have you."

Sienna blushes.

"I want to give her everything I can."

"From what I've seen, you're doing a great job of that. Bree adores you."

"Thank you. That means a lot, especially coming from someone who's so good with her. The way you were with Bree today, making pizza... it was really special."

Warmth spreads through my chest. "She's a great kid. It was fun having you both here today. It's been a long time since this place felt so alive."

For a long time, we sit silently. The sounds of the night disappear as I become acutely aware of Sienna's presence beside me - the gentle rise and fall of her chest as she breathes, the way her fingers absently play with the label on her beer bottle, the subtle scent of her perfume.

She turns toward me.

I lean closer to her. Sienna's breath hitches, her eyes flick to my lips. I can't resist her any longer. I close the distance between us and brush her lips with mine.

Sienna cups my cheek. I wrap my arm around Sienna's waist, pulling her closer. Her lips are soft and warm against mine, and taste of beer and cherries. I lick the seam between her lips and she lets me in.

For a few blissful moments, the world falls away. There is only the warmth of Sienna's mouth as our tongues duel and the softness of her skin under my hand. I lose myself in the kiss, in the feeling of rightness that comes with holding her close.

My cock twitches painfully, straining against my jeans. Needing more, I snake a hand around one plumb breast and squeeze. Sienna moans.

Reality returns. I pull back, shove a hand through my hair, my breathing uneven. "I'm sorry. That shouldn't have happened. I don't want you to think I'm taking advantage of the situation."

Sienna's cheeks are flushed, her eyes bright. Her chest rises and falls rapidly.

"You don't need to apologize. I wanted that as much as you did." She reaches for the crutches and stands. "If I don't leave now, I might take advantage of you."

My heart is pounding. I can't bring myself to smile at her attempt at a joke. I want nothing more than to pull her back into my arms, to lose myself in her warmth and softness. Only, she deserves more than a broken ex-soldier, "Sienna, I..."

"Goodnight, Romeo." She heads inside, leaving me in the company of trees and night creatures.

Chapter 5
SIENNA

THE AROMA OF COFFEE and bacon rouses me from sleep. For a moment, I'm disoriented, the unfamiliar surroundings throwing me off balance. Then it all comes rushing back - the sprained ankle, Romeo's cabin, and that kiss under the stars, the heady sensation created by his hand squeezing my breast. Heat creeps up my neck and face.

I stretch, wincing as I test my ankle. It's still tender, but the swelling has gone down considerably. Romeo's first aid skills are impressive, I have to admit.

I make my way to the kitchen, following the enticing scent of bacon and something sweet. My heart skips a beat at the sight that greets me. Romeo stands at the stove, his back to me, humming softly as he flips pancakes. Bree sits at the table, her legs swinging, as she chatters excitedly.

I'm falling in love with Romeo. His generosity, the way he cares for me and Bree is melting the wall I created around my heart when Bree's dad hurt me. His hair is tied back at his nape.

I stare at the way his muscles strain under his t-shirt. My eyes drop to his butt.

Romeo turns, and the smile he gives me is enough to make my knees weak. "Morning, Sienna. How are you feeling?"

For a second time today, heat suffuses my cheeks.

"Better, thanks to you. Good morning." I hobble to the table. "Something smells amazing."

"Romeo's making chocolate chip pancakes! And bacon!"

"Sounds perfect." I ruffle Bree's hair. "Did you sleep well?"

"I dreamt about the stream. Can we swim?"

I glance at Romeo. He's placing a stack of golden-brown pancakes on the table. "I don't see why not. The water should be warm enough. We can take a picnic."

As we eat breakfast, Romeo tells us about the colorful birds and occasional deer we might see near the stream.

"You're quite the nature expert," I say, impressed by his knowledge.

Romeo shrugs. "I've spent a lot of time exploring these mountains. It helps clear my head."

There's something in his tone, a hint of something deeper, that makes me wonder what exactly he's trying to clear from his head. But before I can dwell on it, Bree tugs at my sleeve, eager to start our adventure.

An hour later, we make our way down a narrow trail towards the stream. Romeo leads the way, carrying a large backpack filled with our picnic supplies and some towels. Bree skips along beside Spot and him, peppering him with questions about every plant and insect we pass. I hobble slowly behind them and enjoy the view - of the lush forest around us and Romeo's broad shoulders in front of me.

The memory of last night's kiss keeps flashing through my mind. Romeo's warm lips, the strength of his arms around me, the way he looked at me in the moonlight - it's all seared into my brain.

"You okay?" Romeo calls over his shoulder.

"I'm fine, just taking in the scenery."

He falls back to walk beside me, letting Bree forge ahead on the clear path. "It's beautiful, isn't it?" He scans the canopy above us. "I never tire of it."

"I can see why." I breathe in the crisp mountain air.

Our hands brush as we walk, sending a jolt of electricity through me. I wonder if he feels it too, this magnetic pull between us. From the way his fingers twitch, as if fighting the urge to grab my hand, I think he might.

It doesn't take long to reach the stream. It's a small, clear blue body of water surrounded by towering pines and a clearing on one side perfect for our picnic.

"Can I go in now?" Bree asks, already pulling off her shoes.

Romeo chuckles. "Go in with mommy and Spot. I'll lay out the food?"

I wore my swimsuit under my clothes, so I just need to slip off my sundress. As I do, I feel Romeo's eyes on me. When I look up, the heat in his gaze makes me shiver despite the warm sun.

Bree races towards the water, and Spot follows her.

"You're not swimming?"

Romeo stares at Bree, then at me, longing in his blue eyes. "I'll be here when you come out."

I follow my little girl and Spot. The water is cool but not unbearable, and soon Bree and I are splashing and laughing.

When we get out of the water, Romeo holds out our towels. As Bree and I dry ourselves, he rubs Spot dry.

After eating the lunch Romeo laid out on the picnic mat, Bree and Spot play on the clearing. The sun is warm on my skin, and I doze off, lulled by the peaceful sounds of nature and Bree's happy giggles.

I'm not sure how long I sleep, but when I wake, the sun has shifted in the sky. Bree is still playing, but Romeo is staring at me.

"Hey, sleepyhead," he whispers, his voice sending a shiver down my spine.

"How long was I out?"

"About an hour. You looked so peaceful; I didn't want to wake you."

I sit and stretch.

His eyes drop to my breasts. My swimming costume, which felt decent this morning, is suddenly tight across my nipples.

"We should probably start packing up." His voice is rougher than usual.

I nod, not trusting my voice. As we gather our things, I wonder what would have happened if Bree hadn't been there.

The walk back to the cabin is quieter than our journey out. Bree is tired from all the excitement, and Romeo and I are lost in our own thoughts. The air between us feels charged. Every accidental touch, every shared glance, feels loaded with meaning.

Back at the cabin, Romeo prepares dinner while I help Bree get cleaned up. As I tuck her into bed later that night, exhausted from our day of adventure, she surprises me with a question.

"Mommy, do you like Romeo?"

I pause, surprised. "Of course I like him, sweetie. He's been very kind to us."

Bree shakes her head, fixing me with a serious look. "No, I mean do you *like* like him? Like how Princess Tiana liked Prince Naveen in the movie?"

My cheeks heat. "It's... complicated, honey. Romeo and I are friends."

I kiss her forehead. "It's time for sleep."

Bree's eyes close yet; as I turn off the light and close the door, her words echo in my mind. Is it that obvious, the way I feel about Romeo?

I make my way back to the living room, but it's empty. Half afraid to sit on the porch with Romeo, I stare at the front door. I'm sure I want a relationship with him, but despite his attraction to me, something is holding him back.

I glance at the bedroom, wondering if I should join Bree. I turn for the porch, needing to know how Romeo is feeling.

The moment I hobble onto the porch, I know something is different. Romeo stands against the railing, body tense. He glances at me, his eyes going to my breasts, reminding me of the way he watched my nipples pebble under my swimming costume earlier in the afternoon.

Suddenly, I'm breathing faster. My mouth goes dry. Without thinking, I try to moisten my lips with the tip of my tongue. Romeo's blue eyes darken as they follow the movement of my pink tongue.

He grabs onto the rails.

I hobble to him, giving him time to move away.

When I'm close enough to touch, he faces me.

There's so much need in his eyes, I can't help standing on my tiptoes and lifting head to kiss him.

"Sienna," Romeo rasps, as if I've tested his patience to the limit.

He picks me up around the waist and as he eases onto the porch swing; I sit on his lap, facing him. I wrap my arms around his neck and brush my lips against him again, desperately needing his touch, momentarily not caring about whether he's willing to commit to me or not.

He nibbles at my mouth, pulling my ass against him.

I almost cry in relief when he finally deepens the kiss and licks on my tongue, drawing on it. His large hands cup my breasts and massage the round globes.

Out of breath, I pull away, then shiver as Romeo takes a nipple into the hot cavern of his mouth. He nips and draws on the hard tip, sending shocks of electricity to my pussy.

I moan, uncaring that my pajama top is getting wet.

I arch my back and pull Romeo to me, holding him at my breast.

He snakes a hand inside my pajama bottoms and panties and strokes my clit. I gyrate against his hand as he steadily increases speed until I'm moaning. He bites my nipple and I explode against his hand, bolts of pleasure vibrating through my body.

Romeo pets the column of my throat until my body goes limp.

Sated, I unbuckle his belt and open the zip of his pants. When I pull the elastic band of his shorts down, his cock rears upward, thick and long, pre-cum oozing from the slit at the head.

I spread the moisture over the head and around the shaft and more pre-cum seeps out.

Romeo grunts. His breaths come faster.

He's so big; I wrap both hands around him and pump up and down his cock. It's been so long since I've done this, I'm uncertain at first, but as Romeo's grunts become more guttural, I pick up speed.

"Yes, Sienna. Like that," he rasps.

He tilts his pelvis forward and buries his hands in my hairs.

I pump faster and harder. His grip tightens on my head, then he's spilling all over my hand. I lean forward, wanting to swallow his come like he did for me, but he holds me back.

I lean against him. His arms wrap around me.

The night air cools, making me shiver.

"Let me take you inside," Romeo says.

"To your room?"

"No!"

Chapter 6

SIENNA

I FROWN. THE DENIAL in Romeo's voice is strong. Unease fills me.

"What's the matter?"

Romeo stands up with me in his arms and puts me down inside the cabin.

"I'm sorry, Sienna. I shouldn't have done that. You deserve a man who can give you a future, and I'm not that man."

"I like you, Romeo. I'm in love with you. Maybe if we give this a chance, it might work."

He shakes his head.

"Sienna, I want to have you and Bree permanently in my life. I want to see your belly grow with my baby. I want you so bad, I'm going crazy with it. But you deserve better."

"Tell me why you believe you're not enough."

He stares at me for a long time, but he shakes his head and steps outside, shutting the door to the cabin.

I stare at the door, frustrated and sad.

When I open the door, he's no longer on the porch or in the front of the cabin.

I head back inside and wash up. I toss and turn the entire night; glad Bree is a heavy sleeper. Finally, in the early hours of the morning, I fall asleep.

I wake up before Bree. The smell of pancakes and bacon leads me to the kitchen. But Romeo is not there.

He's left a note saying to eat breakfast and the lunch he left in the fridge, that he'll come back after lunch, to take us home.

"Do you know where your daddy is?" I ask Spot.

The mutt looks at me with a soulful expression, then licks my face.

Bree and I spend the morning outside, in the clearing in front of the cabin. I can't concentrate on the book I brought, even though I was looking forward to it. Every now and again, Bree looks towards the trees, and I can tell she misses Romeo.

We have lunch in the cabin and pack our bags.

"When is Romeo coming? Did he write he'll take us home, Mommy?"

"He'll be here soon. He said after lunch, and we finished eating only a while ago."

Spot barks and races to the door. Bree follows the dog and is just as excited to see Romeo walk in.

He ruffles her hair

"Are you taking us home?" She asks.

"I am. Are you ready?"

"We are," I say from the door of the bedroom.

"I'll take your backpack. Take the crutches."

How can he care so much and not be willing to try a relationship?

He puts out belongings in the truck and helps Bree up onto the back seat, strapping her in. Spot jumps in beside her.

On the porch, I hesitate, reluctant to leave. Romeo comes up to me.

"Can we talk?"

He shakes his head, not meeting my eyes. "There's nothing to talk about, Sienna. You deserve someone who can give you everything, who doesn't have a past that haunts them. That's not me."

"You don't get to decide what I deserve," I say, frustration and hurt warring in my chest. "I'm not asking for perfection, Romeo. I'm just asking for a chance."

He finally looks at me then, and the pain in his eyes takes my breath away. "I can't give you what you need, Sienna. I thought maybe I could, but I can't."

He heads to the car, opens the passenger door and waits until I'm sitting before going round to the driver's seat and heading out.

He asks Bree if she enjoyed her weekend and keeps a steady chat of conversations with her. His consideration for her only makes me sadder because it reinforces what a great dad he'd make. Even though things are strained between us, he'd doing everything he can to ensure Bree doesn't realize that and become sad.

Romeo insists on helping me up the stairs to our apartment, his hand on my elbow steadying me as I navigate the steps with my still-tender ankle. He carries my backpack, setting it down gently just inside the door, then stands outsides, on the doorstep.

Bree hugs him and Spot, longing in her eyes.

"Wait inside, sweetie. I'm just going to thank Romeo for letting us stay in his cabin."

I wait until she enters her bedroom, then turn to the man in front of me.

"Thank you so much for taking care of us. We had a lovely time."

"I'm glad," Romeo says softly. "You're both... you're very special to me. I hope you know that."

Special, but not special enough. Not enough for him to take a chance, to let me in.

"I'm sorry, Sienna," he says suddenly, his voice raw. "I wish I could be the man you need me to be. The man you deserve. But I'm not sure I know how to be that man anymore."

My heart clenches at his words, at the vulnerability in his eyes. "Romeo, your past doesn't define you. What defines you is how you choose to move forward. And the man I see in front of me, the man who's been so wonderful with Bree, who makes me feel things I haven't felt in years... that's a good man. A man worth taking a chance on."

For a moment, I think I see a flicker of hope in his eyes, a crack in the armor. But then it's gone, replaced by a steely resolve. "I'm sorry. I can't be that man. Not right now. Maybe never. And you deserve more than maybes."

The finality in his tone, the set of his jaw, tells me there's no changing his mind. Not today. Maybe never, just like he said.

"I should probably get going. Let you and Bree settle back in."

"Goodbye, Romeo."

"Goodbye, Sienna."

For a moment, I think he's going to say more, but then he turns and goes down the stairs. I feel like a part of my heart goes with him.

I close the door. Bree comes up beside me, slipping her little hand into mine. "Are you okay, Mommy?"

I look at her, forcing a smile. "I will be, sweetie. It's just... complicated."

"Are we going to see Romeo and Spot again?" she asks, eyes huge.

I pull her into my arms, hugging her close. "I don't know, baby, hopefully."

"I miss them already."

"Me too."

As I stand there, holding my daughter, I feel a profound sense of loss. In just a few short days, Romeo and his cabin in the mountains had felt like home, like a future I hadn't even known I was longing for.

But now, with the echoes of his goodbye still ringing in my ears and the memory of the pain in his eyes haunting me, that future seems further away than ever.

And as much as it hurts, as much as every part of me wants to chase after him, to demand that he face his fears and give us a shot, I know I can't. I have to let him go, have to trust that if we're meant to be, he'll find his way back to me.

Until then, I have to be strong. For Bree, for me.

I take a deep breath and square my shoulders.

"Come on, sweetie. Let's unpack. Maybe we can go to the park, eh? We can feed the ducks, just like you love to do."

"Can we get ice cream after?"

"Yes. Let's end our weekend trip with a treat."

As I bustle around the apartment, unpacking our bags, I ignore the ache in my chest, and focus on being the best mom I can be for Bree.

Chapter 7
ROMEO

AS I DRIVE AWAY from Sienna's apartment, every part of my being screams at me to go back. But I keep driving away from Blossom, my mind reeling, my heart aching with the weight of my decision. I drive for hours, unable to face my empty cabin.

When I finally arrive home, it's dark and I'm surprised to find Riker waiting for me on the porch. He's one of my closest friends and a member of my team.

"We need to move forward with the rescue operation for Lori and her mom. I think her dad has figured out they are trying to escape." Riker says.

My mind shifts into work mode. This is what I'm good at, what I'm trained for. Helping those who can't help themselves.

As Riker fills me in on the details, I can't help but think of how Sienna looked at me with trust in her eyes and the way Bree's laughter filled the cabin, bringing light to every corner. I want to protect them from any danger.

We agree on a date to carry out the rescue operation.

"Something is on your mind," Riker says. "Is this about the woman that stayed over this weekend?"

"I took her and her daughter home."

"And now, you're dissing yourself about it."

"They deserve more than I can give them. I'm not the man they need."

"Bullshit! You're the best man I know, Rome. And if you keep letting your past hold you back, you're going to miss out on someone special."

His words hit me like a punch to the gut. Because deep down, I know he's right. Being with Sienna and Bree, letting myself care for them... it felt right in a way few things ever have.

"What if my legs scare her away?"

Riker claps a hand on my shoulder. "What if she doesn't? Brave up, man, and give her a chance to decide for herself."

Am I any different from Bree's father? Just like he did, I'm not putting her first. My fear of rejection is above all else. And that's just wrong.

I take a deep breath and exhale slowly. Sienna comes first. That means I must find the courage to show her who I am and let her decide if she's willing to have me.

"Thanks Riker," I say to his back as he sprints off.

I have to see Sienna. I get back in my truck, drive down the mountain at a breakneck speed. As drive past Jackson's Diner, I'm forced to slow down, to avoid hitting the families coming out after the dinner rush, but my foot hits the gas again as move away from the restaurant.

When I arrive at Sienna's apartment, my heart is pounding. I knock on the door, my palms sweaty, my mouth dry.

Sienna opens the door, surprise in her eyes.

"I need to talk to you," I say, my voice rough with emotion. "Please, Sienna. It's important."

She hesitates for a moment, then steps aside to let me in. "Bree's asleep. We can talk in the living room."

"I need to show you something. In the bedroom."

Sienna's eyes widen, but she nods.

In the bedroom, I take deep breaths, trying to calm my racing heart. "Sienna, there's something I haven't told you. Something I've been afraid to show you."

"What is it?"

Quickly, with shaking hands, I strip my bottom half to my shorts. The metal of my prosthetics gleams in the bedroom light, the artificial limbs a stark contrast to the skin on the rest of my body.

I hear Sienna's sharp intake of breath, and I close my eyes, bracing myself for her reaction. For the disgust, the pity, the rejection.

"You're breathing a little too fast. What's the matter?"

I open my eyes and look at her. There's only concern in her gaze. "Are you worried about my breathing right now?"

"What else should I be worried about?"

I sit, remove both my prosthetic legs, and place them on the floor. My heart rate is speeding up, despite all the damned training I've had on regulating breathing.

"This is me." I point to my stumps, roughly half-way below my knees.

"You're gorgeous," Sienna says after a while.

I stare at, not sure I heard right.

"Can I touch them?"

Her rich brown eyes are as warm as they were throughout the weekend. My breathing eases a little. I nod.

She scoots closer to me. With both hands, she caresses the rough skin around my residual limbs.

"Does it hurt?"

"No." My voice is hoarse, charged with emotion.

"Can you feel it?"

"Sienna..."

"Tell me how you feel about my legs."

She looks at me.

"You don't have any pain. I know little about amputations, but the skin looks good to me. Your thighs are strong too and by the way you were moving all weekend, it looks to me like you've mastered using your prosthetics. It's like they're a part of you. I'm awed."

"And?"

Her face scrunches up. "Are you asking if I'm okay being with you, despite your amputated legs?"

"Yes."

"I want you more than I did yesterday. Because you had the guts to show me all of you. I love your powerful arms and thighs, the way you make me scream with pleasure and get turned on just by looking at you but, I love your mental strength, compassion and the way you cared for me and Bree even more."

The weight on my chest lifts.

"I love you," I say, looking into her brown eyes.

She looks at me searchingly.

"Will you go out with me?"

"Yes."

I pull her toward me. I meant to kiss her reverently; to show her how much her words mean to me but the moment my lips touch hers, a fierce hunger surges through me.

Sienna bites my bottom lip.

I groan. "If you do that again, you'll find yourself naked with me inside you in no time. We should probably go on a few dates before we do that, right?."

She rubs her hand across my burgeoning dick.

"Your little strip made me horny. So, I'll need either you or BOB tonight. I choose you."

I still.

"Bob?"

Chapter 8
SIENNA

"MY BATTERY-OPERATED BOYFRIEND. My vibrator."

Romeo groans. He pulls my hands away from him and holds them behind my back.

"I almost came in my pants," he rasps out, eyes hot with need.

"I want you to feel that way. I can't stop thinking about how good it felt when you touched me on the porch."

"Keep your hands behind your back, unless I tell you otherwise."

I nod.

Romeo opens the buttons on my pajama top. I shiver as his hands brush against my sensitive skin. He moistens his lips as he pushes the top off me, exposing my breasts.

He pulls my bottoms and panties down and I lift my bottom off the bed, watching as he slides the materials down my thighs and knees until they pool at my feet.

I move back on the bed and lie down, staring at him, hoping he likes my saggy middle.

"You're beautiful, Sienna," his voice catches.

He removes his shorts, lies beside me, and places my arms above my head.

"I want to touch you," I say.

"Later. I can't control myself right now. I want our first time to be good for you."

Before I can say we have all the time in the world, he slides his tongue into my mouth. Each glide sends heat down to my core. I moan, tilting my head for an even deeper kiss.

Romeo massages one breast, his fingers rolling the tip. Electricity arches down my belly and moisture seeps out of me. He nips at my earlobe, causing tiny shocks of pleasure to shoot through my body.

I bring my arms down, wanting to press his head to me.

He lifts his head, the heat in his gaze driving me higher.

"Don't stop."

"Put them back."

As soon as I do, Romeo pets my other earlobe, making me moan again and wonder if I'm going to come without him touching my aching, increasingly wet pussy.

"I love the way your skin smells, baby."

He blows on the earlobe he just sucked, and I shiver.

He peppers hot, wet kisses down my throat, then takes one pebbled nipple into the heat of his mouth, sucking hard on it, as he rolls the other nipple.

I come apart, my core clenching again and again as pleasure lances through my body.

"You look lovely when you come."

Romeo glides on top of me and kisses me, his hands cupping my cheeks. I glide my hands down his back, loving the way his chest crushes my breasts, and stroke the round globes of his buttocks. I reach between us and touch his thick, hard length, spreading the moisture on the tip of his cock throughout the head.

Romeo groans and moves out of my reach.

He slides down my body and kisses my belly button before stationing himself between my legs.

"It's too soon." I try to pull him up my body. It's no use. He must weigh upwards of two-hundred-pounds and it's all muscle.

"It isn't."

Leisurely, like he's eating a lollipop, he licks my clit. Then he inserts his tongue into my channel, fucking me slowly with his tongue.

Heat builds inside me again.

Romeo replaces removes his tongue out of me and inserts his fingers, scissoring them. He sucks on my swelling clit, pulling on the soft flesh.

I dig my nails into his back as his mouth pulls harder and his fingers speed up. I'm moaning again as pleasure surges inside of me once again.

"That's it, baby. Come for me again," Romeo rasps against my engorged flesh and squeezes my butt cheeks.

My body convulses, as waves of pleasure wash over me, so strong that my eyes shut.

He moves up my body.

"Baby, open your eyes. I want your eyes on me as I enter your body."

Romeo's cock presses against my entrance. I open my eyes and gaze into his deep blue eyes.

He stares back into my eyes.

"I love you, Sienna."

"I love you too, Romeo. My Romeo."

He tucks his hands under my ass and penetrates me, his long, thick shaft tunneling through the constricting walls of my pussy.

I arch under the invasion, loving the sensation of fullness, and wrap my legs around him, bringing him deeper into me.

Romeo lifts out of me almost to the tip, before thrusting back in and burying himself to the hilt. He fucks me hard, each stroke faster until I'm keening, my body begging for release again.

He buries his mouth in my neck and I hold him close, needing as much of our skin touching as possible.

He stills, then grunts as he jerks into me, his seed shooting into my pussy and I come again with a cry, my vagina contracting uncontrollably.

Romeo puts his mouth on mine, swallowing my cry.

I must have fallen asleep because when I open my eyes, Romeo is on his back and I'm lying against his side, his arms wrapped tight around me.

I look up to find him staring at me.

"Did I wake Bree?"

He smiles. "The walls must be good or she's a heavy sleeper."

"She's a heavy sleeper, but I'm not used to having anyone over."

"I checked. She's sleeping."

I stare at him, gratitude filling me.

"What?"

"I'm wondering what I did to deserve you. I'm happy. Bree will be too."

He brushes a lock of tightly curled black hair away from my face.

"You accepted and loved me as I am. I will not take you for granted. I'll always put you and Bree first. I almost lost you because I didn't share my deepest fear with you. I won't do that anymore."

I pet his beard, moved by the sincerity in his eyes. "Me too. I promise not to take you for granted and put you and Bree first."

Epilogue

ROMEO

One Year later

THE SUN IS JUST beginning to set over the mountains, painting the sky a brilliant array of oranges and pinks. I stand on the porch of my cabin, nervously adjusting my tie for the hundredth time. Today's the day, the moment I've been planning for months. The moment I ask Sienna to be mine forever.

I glance over at the yard where our friends and family are gathered. Bonnie and Rory are setting up the refreshments table, laughing and teasing each other as they work. Riker is entertaining Bree and some of the other kids with his silly magic tricks. And Sienna's best friends, Scarlett, Destiny, and Rosa, are huddled together, whispering and giggling like schoolgirls.

My heart swells with love and gratitude for these people, this makeshift family we've created. A year ago, I never could have imagined my life would look like this. But now, I can't imagine it any other way.

IRIS WEST

The sound of a car pulling up draws my attention, and I feel my pulse kick into overdrive. Sienna. She thinks she's coming over for a simple barbecue, a celebration of our one-year anniversary. She has no idea what I really have planned.

I watch as she steps out of the car, gorgeous as always in a flowy sundress, her hair tumbling down her back in soft waves. Bree bounds over to her, chattering excitedly, and Sienna laughs, hugging her close.

I make my way down the porch steps, my eyes locked on Sienna. When she sees me, her face lights up in that special smile she reserves just for me.

"Hey, handsome," she says as I reach her, leaning in for a kiss. "Happy anniversary."

"Happy anniversary," I murmur against her lips. "I can't believe it's been a year already."

"The best year of my life," she breathes, her eyes shining with love.

I take her hand, lacing our fingers together. "Mine too. And I'm hoping for many more to come."

I lead her into the yard, where everyone greets her with hugs and good wishes. As the barbecue gets underway, I get more and more nervous. I keep reaching into my pocket, feeling the small velvet box hidden there.

Finally, as the sun dips below the horizon, it's time. I catch Destiny's eye, and she nods, a conspiratorial smile on her face.

She knows what I have planned, has been helping me orchestrate this moment for weeks.

"Can I have a moment, please? There's something I need to say."

All eyes turn to me, curious and expectant. I take a deep breath, turning to face Sienna. Her eyes widen as I sink down on one knee before her, pulling the ring box from my pocket.

"Sienna," I begin, my voice shaking slightly. "A year ago, you stumbled into my life and changed everything. You showed me what it means to love and be loved wholly and unconditionally. You gave me a family, a home, a future I never thought I could have."

Sienna clasps her hands over her mouth. Around us, our friends and family have fallen silent.

"I love you, Sienna. Your strength, kindness and unwavering faith in me amaze me. I love the way you love Bree, the way you've opened your heart to me. I want to wake up next to you every morning and fall asleep with you in my arms every night."

I open the ring box, revealing the simple but elegant diamond solitaire inside. Sienna gasps.

"I want to spend the rest of my life loving you, Sienna. I want to build a future with you, watch Bree grow up and have kids of our own, face every challenge and celebrate every joy with you by my side."

I take a deep breath, my heart in my throat. "Sienna Washington, will you marry me?"

For a moment, there's silence. Then, with a sob of joy, Sienna launches herself into my arms, almost knocking us both to the ground. "Yes," she cries, peppering my face with kisses. "Yes, yes, a thousand times, yes!"

Around us, our friends and family erupt into cheers and applause. Bree comes running over, throwing herself on top of us in a giggling heap. "Does this mean Romeo's going to be my daddy for real now?" she asks, her face lit up with excitement.

"It sure does, munchkin," I say, hugging her close. "Is that okay with you?"

"It's more than okay!" Bree exclaims. "It's the best thing ever!"

As we untangle ourselves and get to our feet, Sienna holds out her shaking hand so I can slide the ring onto her finger. It fits perfectly, just like I knew it would. Just like Sienna fits perfectly into my life, my heart.

The rest of the evening passes in a blur of congratulations, happy tears, and clinking glasses. Bonnie and Rory insist on making a toast, regaling everyone with embarrassing stories of my love-struck behavior over the past year. Riker pulls me into a bone-crushing hug, telling me how proud he is of the man I've become. And Sienna's friends gather around her, admiring her ring and already planning her bachelorette party.

But through it all, my eyes keep straying back to my fiancée, the love of my life. She catches me looking and smiles, her eyes soft and full of promise. We have a lot of planning to do, a wedding to organize and a future to build. But right now, in this moment, all that matters is that she said yes. She chose me, just like I've chosen her, forever and always.

After the night winds down and our guests depart, Sienna and I wind up on the porch swing, Bree fast asleep in my lap. Sienna leans her head on my shoulder, her hand resting on my chest, right over my heart.

"I love you," she whispers, her voice thick with emotion. "I can't wait to be your wife."

"I love you too," I murmur back, pressing a kiss to her temple. "More than I ever thought possible."

We sit there for a long time, listening to the crickets chirp and watching the stars twinkle overhead. And as I hold my family close, feeling the steady beat of Sienna's heart against my side and the soft weight of Bree in my arms, I know I'm exactly where I'm meant to be.

Because this, right here? This is what happily ever after looks like. And I wouldn't trade it for anything in the world.

SINGLE MOM AND THE BILLIONAIRE

BLOSSOM FORD MOMS BOOK 2

IRIS WEST

Chapter 1
JASPER

WATCHING DESTINY THROUGH THE glass wall of my office has become one of my favorite pastimes, which is dangerous when it's only ten on a Wednesday morning and I am supposed to be working instead of controlling the boner in my pants. I shift in my chair and breathe deeply but can't tear my gaze from the sight of her even front teeth worrying her luscious bottom lip–a sure sign she's trying to figure out a solution to a problem.

Her fingers are hidden by the laptop in front of her, but from the way she's sitting, they must be moving at the speed of light. Her oval-shaped face is focused on the screen, the smoothness of her chocolate milk skin marred by her scrunched nose. She's doing what I pay her to do, being a damn good personal assistant, despite her young age of twenty-five.

From the moment she marched into my office for her interview in a color block striped pantsuit that fit her curvy breasts and ass like a glove twenty-one months ago, I fell in lust. She was the most beautiful woman I'd ever seen. She was younger and less experienced than the other candidates shortlisted, but after the personal assistant who'd started out as my father's secretary retired, I'd instructed Human Resources that a passion for logistics and automated processes was my priority.

Thirty minutes into the interview, I knew she was the woman I'd been looking for all my life. Like me, she'd learned a lot about managing the movement of goods from her father, who was in the military. For the first time in my life, a woman's mind turned me on.

As if sensing my scrutiny, she glances toward me. Catches me staring. Instead of pressing the intercom and making up something, like I've done every time I've been caught red-handed, I carry on watching her for a few beats, my longing for her clear. Hiding the fact I want her has been hell.

Her teeth worry her bottom lip again, and I almost groan. I clear my throat and press a button.

"Come into the office in fifteen minutes with the data I requested." I'm glad I can control my voice.

"Yes, Mr. Cleveland."

She insists on calling me that. And each time, it reminds me I'm ten years older than her. Yet, the way she says it with her slightly husky voice sounds like an endearment.

I force myself to focus on work and by the time she knocks on my door, enters the office and sits herself down on the chair across my desk, my body is under control.

Cleveland Logistics recently gained a major client, so Destiny and I spend the rest of the morning going over everything that needs to be in place when we take over transporting their goods.

Working with her excites me. I love pitting myself against her razor-sharp mind.

"How is Aiden?" I ask before she stands. Her two-year-old boy was unwell a few days ago.

Her eyes light up. The most gorgeous dimples appear on her cheeks as she smiles and I want to mean as much to her as her little boy does, to be one of her treasured people.

"Much better. I took him to daycare. Thank you for asking."

"I do the same for every employee."

I remember they have kids, but rarely do I remember the kids' names. Not only do I remember Destiny's boy's name, but also the toys and food he likes.

"It's great how you remember everyone's names. Even the drivers. That's more than a thousand names!"

"It helps that I met some of them when I visited my father's office during summer breaks and some others went to my school."

Desire simmers beneath my skin as I drink in the sight of her. I'm not blind to the differences between us. The decade that separates us in age, the chasm in wealth and status. She's a young single mother just hitting her stride in her career. I'm a jaded billionaire at the helm of an empire. On paper, we make no sense. But my mind and body want Destiny. And I'm not a man who backs down from what he wants.

I've bid my time, giving Destiny space to heal from her divorce and adjust to single motherhood. She needed time, so I watched over her from a careful distance. But I've noticed a change in her the last couple of months. I'm done holding myself in check.

It's pure torture being this close to her, inhaling her sweet vanilla scent, and not being able to reach out and touch. To trail my fingers along the graceful curve of her neck, to loosen her ponytail and bury my nose in her locs and just breathe her in. I've never wanted a woman the way I want Destiny.

I want to worship her luscious body until she's trembling and crying for my name. I want to shatter her defenses, tear down her walls brick by brick, until she knows that she's the center of my whole damn world.

As she looks at me, I let my guard slip for just a moment. I let her see the hunger in my eyes, the intensity of my focus on her. Her breath catches and a flush stains her cheeks. My cock twitches at the sight, hard and heavy behind my zipper.

Chapter 2
DESTINY

AS I SIT ACROSS from Jasper, discussing Aiden's health and marveling at the way he remembers the names of all his employees, a flare of attraction lights up in my belly. It's not the first time I've noticed how handsome he is, with his chiseled jaw, piercing hazel eyes, and the sexy scruff that shadows his chin.

When I first met Jasper during my job interview, I was immediately struck by his good looks, his height of well over six feet, and commanding presence. But I was in no headspace to even consider acting on my attraction. I had just gone through a brutal divorce from Aiden's father, my college sweetheart, mere months after giving birth. My world had been turned upside down, my dreams of a perfect little family shattered by his betrayal. All I could focus on was survival, on providing for myself and my infant son.

Landing this job at Cleveland Logistics had been a godsend. Not only was the pay incredible, but the benefits were top-notch and the office was just minutes from Aiden's daycare.

I'd be able to support my little boy while still being there for all his important milestones. It was more than I could have hoped for as a newly single mom.

I'd respected Jasper Cleveland long before I met him in person. The innovative changes he'd made to his family's company after taking over from his late father were industry legend. He'd taken a successful but somewhat stagnant business and turned it into an innovative powerhouse in just a few short years. When I applied for the personal assistant position, I thought at most it would be an excellent learning experience, a chance to glimpse the brilliant CEO in action.

I never dreamed my hodgepodge of experience - the logistics internships I'd done during college summers, the six months I'd spent at a trucking competitor before following my ex to Blossom Ford, and the nuggets of wisdom I'd picked up from my dad and brother during their military careers - would be enough to land me the job. But Jasper saw something in me, a glimmer of potential and a hunger to learn that set me apart from the other candidates. He challenges me intellectually and values my opinions.

And now, nearly two years later, I'm sitting in his office, discussing the minutiae of his schedule. I admire Jasper for so much more than his business acumen. His compassion for his employees, his dedication to his family's legacy, and his incisive mind have all earned my deep respect and loyalty.

But lately, my feelings have shifted into more dangerous territory. I've caught myself watching the way his muscles move beneath his tailored suits, admiring the confident set of his shoulders and the way his long fingers wrap around his coffee mug. At night, alone in my bed, my mind drifts into fantasies of those hands on my body, those lips trailing fire across my skin.

I try to shake off those thoughts, to bury them deep. Jasper is my boss, and a billionaire to boot. He could have any woman he wants - a model, an heiress, someone glamorous and cultured and whole. Not a single mom with stretch marks and a toddler.

But then there are moments, fleeting glances and loaded pauses, that make me wonder if I'm imagining the heat in his eyes when he looks at me. Like today, when he'd stared at me across the office with such intensity, it stole my breath. Or last week, when his hand brushed mine as he passed me a file and I swear I felt a jolt of electricity between us.

My friends have noticed it too. Rosa keeps telling me that Jasper is always finding excuses to swing by my desk, that his eyes follow me whenever I'm turned away. And Scarlett, who knows the retired personal assistant, swears he's never been this hands-on with an assistant before, that he seems to enjoy my company beyond just a professional capacity.

I brush off their comments, afraid to get my hopes up. They're seeing what they want to see, projecting their own romantic notions onto two people who work closely together. That's all this is - a boss and his assistant, forming a close working relationship. To think it could be anything more is pure fantasy.

Besides, even if by some miracle Jasper was interested in me that way, I can't go down that road again. I barely survived having my heart shattered by Aiden's father when he cheated on me just months into our marriage. The pain of that betrayal still takes my breath away sometimes.

I can't risk that kind of heartbreak again, not when I have Aiden to think about. My sweet boy needs stability, not a mother who's pining after an unattainable man. I have to focus on being the best parent I can be, on giving my son the loving, consistent home he deserves.

No, it's better to keep my silly crush hidden, to bury it deep and keep things professional with Jasper. I have too much to lose - this amazing job that keeps a roof over our heads, the comfortable rhythm I've found as a working single mom. I won't jeopardize all that for the sake of some far-fetched daydreams.

Jasper is my boss, and that's all he can ever be. A kind, intelligent, drop-dead sexy boss. But still just a boss.

I'll have to content myself with admiring him from afar, with the fantasies I spin in the dark of night. That's as close as I'll ever get to the enigmatic billionaire who sets my heart racing.

Chapter 3

JASPER

WORKING WITH DESTINY TODAY has been both heaven and hell. Heaven, because every moment spent in her presence is a gift, a chance to bask in her warmth and brilliance. And hell, because the simmering attraction between us is becoming harder to ignore with each passing hour.

There's a charge in the air, a crackling tension that sets my nerve endings alight. It's in the accidental brush of our fingers as we pass documents back and forth, the lingering glances when we think the other isn't looking. I've caught her watching me with a heat in her eyes that mirrors my own, and it takes every ounce of my self-control not to sweep her into my arms and claim her lips with a searing kiss.

But I hold back, knowing that Destiny needs to be the one to make the first move. After the way her ex betrayed her, I wouldn't be surprised if she were wary of letting another man into her heart. I need to prove to her I'm different, that my feelings for her are real and unshakable.

As the day winds down and the office empties, I seize my chance to spend a little extra time with her.

"Destiny, could you come into my office for a moment?"

She appears in the doorway, her curvy figure silhouetted against the soft light of the setting sun streaming through the windows. "Yes, Mr. Cleveland?"

I gesture for her to take a seat, trying to calm the nervous energy thrumming through my veins. "I wanted to talk to you about the transition with the new client; I'm a little concerned about some processes we have in place."

Destiny's brow furrows as she leans forward, her brilliant mind already whirring with solutions. "What specifically are you worried about?"

We dive into the details, bouncing ideas back and forth as we try to troubleshoot the potential hiccups. But even as we're deep in discussion, I can't help but be distracted by the way the light dances across her smooth milk chocolate skin, the fullness of her lips as she talks.

God, I want to kiss her.

I shake my head, trying to focus on the task at hand. "I think we're going to need to put in some extra hours to get this sorted before the handoff next week. Are you up for a late night or two?"

Destiny sighs, her shoulders slumping slightly. "I want to say yes, but I need to figure out childcare for Aiden first. My usual babysitter has finals this week. I'll have to see if my friends can help."

My heart clenches at the weariness in her voice. I hate seeing her stretched so thin, torn between her duties as a mother and her dedication to her job.

An idea takes shape in my mind, a way to kill two birds with one stone. "What if we worked from your place tonight? That way, Aiden can sleep in his own bed and we can still tackle this problem."

Destiny bites her lip, hesitation flickering in her dark eyes. "I don't know. It's not exactly professional for my boss to come over to my apartment at night."

I lean forward, holding her gaze with mine. "Destiny, I would do nothing to make you uncomfortable or jeopardize our working relationship. I respect you far too much for that."

She nods, but I can still see the uncertainty clouding her features.

"I promise I won't do anything you don't want me to."

"And what about Aiden? He can be a handful when he's overtired."

"Aiden and I are friends, remember? We bonded over our shared love of chocolate chip cookies and trucks at the O'Connors' St. Patrick's Day picnic. And he always sneaks into our video chats when you're working from home."

Destiny laughs, the sound warming me from the inside out. "He remembers 'Mr. Japper' whenever he's eating chocolate chip cookies. And he keeps asking when 'Mr. Japper' is going over to play trucks with him again."

"Then it's settled. I'll swing by around seven with dinner. Does pizza work? I think you inhaled three slices at the company picnic."

"Hey, I was breastfeeding. That burns a lot of calories."

I throw my hands up in surrender, chuckling. "No judgment here. I admire the way you take care of Aiden, yet work so hard for the company."

The air between us shifts, the playfulness giving way to something deeper, more intimate. Destiny holds my gaze, a softness stealing into her eyes that makes my breath catch.

"Thank you, Mr. Cleveland, for understanding. It means a lot to me."

"Thank you for being an excellent personal assistant." *Thank you for coming into my life.*

For a moment, there's this undeniable pull between us. Then the spell is broken.

"I should head out and get Aiden from daycare. I'll see you soon."

Chapter 4
DESTINY

I CAN'T BELIEVE I agreed to let Jasper come over to my apartment tonight. It feels like crossing a line, blurring the boundaries between our professional and personal lives.

But as I remind myself, this isn't the first time we've worked together outside of the office. There have been plenty of late nights in hotel rooms - during business trips - poring over contracts and spreadsheets until the small hours of the morning.

Through it all, Jasper has been a consummate professional. Never once has he made me feel uncomfortable or overstepped any boundaries.

And if I'm being honest with myself, the idea of spending an evening with him outside of work sends a thrill of excitement through me. I've been fighting my growing attraction to him for months now, telling myself it's just a harmless crush. But lately, it's been getting harder to ignore the way my pulse races when he looks at me, the way my skin tingles when he brushes against me.

I shake my head, pushing those dangerous thoughts aside. I can't go down that road, no matter how tempting it may be.

With a newfound sense of resolve, I gather my things and head out to pick up Aiden from daycare. The moment I step through the doors of Smart Teddies, my heart melts at the sight of my baby boy toddling towards me with a gummy grin.

"Mama!" he squeals, throwing his chubby arms around my legs.

I scoop him up and cover his face in kisses, breathing in his sweet baby scent. "Hi, love. Did you have a good day?"

Aiden chuckles and chatters about his day, his hands gesturing as we make our way to the car.

Back at the apartment, I go through the familiar motions of bath time and dinner prep, trying to ignore the nervous energy humming beneath my skin. As I chop vegetables for a salad, I find myself second-guessing my outfit choice - a simple pair of jeans and a burnt orange blouse.

"It's just Jasper. He's seen you in sweatpants and a messy bun around town."

But even as I say the words, I know they're a lie. This is different. Having Jasper in my home, playing with my son, feels intimate in a way that makes my heart race and my palms sweat.

A knock at the door startles me out of my thoughts. I take a deep breath, smoothing my hair and tugging at my blouse before opening the door to reveal a grinning Jasper, his arms laden with pizza boxes.

"Someone order a large pepperoni with extra cheese?" he teases, his hazel eyes sparkling with mirth.

"Mister Japper!" Aiden barrels past me, launching himself at Jasper's legs with an excited squeal.

Jasper laughs, carefully balancing the pizza boxes as he reaches down to ruffle Aiden's curls. "Hey buddy."

Aiden bounces on his toes as Jasper steps inside. I watch in amusement as my baby boy leads my boss to the kitchen table, chattering away about his day at daycare.

"I hope pepperoni is okay." Jasper sets the boxes on the table.

"Any pizza is always a hit in the Turner household. Although I'm attempting to balance it out with some vegetables, for the sake of my waistline."

Jasper's gaze rakes over my figure, a hint of heat flickering in his eyes. "Trust me, your waistline is perfect just the way it is."

I flush at the compliment, my stomach flipping pleasantly. Before I can respond, Aiden tugs at Jasper's hand, demanding his attention.

"Mister Japper, come see my trucks!"

Jasper allows himself to be led into the living room. "Lead the way, little man. Let's see how fast we can make them go."

As I watch them play, my heart swells with an emotion I'm afraid to name. They look so natural together, so at ease in each other's company. For a moment, I let myself imagine what it would be like if this were our everyday reality - coming home to Jasper, watching him bond with my son, sharing meals and laughter and love.

I shake my head, pushing the fantasy aside.

Dinner is a lively affair, with Aiden regaling us with toddler-speak stories. By the time we've polished off the pizza and salad, my cheeks ache from laughing so much.

"Alright, little man, time for bed." I scoop Aiden up and pepper his face with kisses.

"No, Mama," he whines, wriggling in my arms. "Want Mister Japper to read the story?"

I glance at Jasper uncertainly, but he's already rising from his seat. "I'd be happy to help with bedtime duties. If that's okay with you, Destiny?"

My heart skips a beat at the tenderness in his voice. "Of course. Aiden would love that."

Together, we go through the familiar routine of pajamas and toothbrushing, Aiden's eyelids drooping with each passing minute. By the time we settle in for story-time, he's curled up in my lap, fighting to keep his eyes open.

Jasper sits beside us on the bed, his deep voice soothing as he reads about a little engine that could fly. I get lost in the rumble of his words, the warmth of his presence beside me.

In that moment, with my son heavy in my arms and Jasper's shoulder brushing against mine, I feel a sense of rightness, of belonging. This is what I've been missing, what I've been craving deep down in my bones.

A family. A partner. Someone to share the joys and burdens of parenthood with.

But as quickly as the feeling comes, it's gone, replaced by a sharp pang of longing. Because Jasper isn't mine.

Aiden's soft snores fill the room as Jasper closes the book, a tender smile playing at his lips. Together, we tuck him into bed, our hands brushing as we smooth the covers over his small body.

The touch sends a jolt of electricity through me, and I snatch my hand back as if burned. Jasper's eyes find mine in the dim light, a question brewing in their brown-green depths.

But I look away, my heart racing as I lead him out of the room and back to the living room. We have work to do, problems to solve.

We settle in at the table, our shoulders hunched over laptops and papers as we dive into the logistics of the new client handoff. But even as we discuss routing schedules and inventory tracking, I can feel the tension crackling between us, the unspoken words hanging heavy in the air.

It's nearing midnight by the time we finally come up for air, our eyes bleary from staring at screens for so long. Jasper stretches, his shirt riding up to reveal a strip of tanned skin that makes my mouth go dry.

"I think we've made some good progress." His voice is husky with fatigue. "But we should probably call it a night. I don't want to keep you up any later."

I suddenly feel awkward and unsure. The easy camaraderie of the evening has given way to something else, something charged and heavy with possibility.

Jasper stands, gathering his things as he prepares to leave. But as he turns to face me, his eyes lock onto mine with an intensity that steals my breath.

"Destiny. I..."

He trails off, shaking his head as if thinking better of whatever he was about to say. I swallow, my heart pounding in my throat.

"Thank you for tonight," I say, my voice barely above a whisper. "For everything. I know it wasn't the most conventional work arrangement, but I appreciate your flexibility."

Jasper takes a step closer, his gaze never leaving mine. "I meant what I said earlier. I would do nothing to make you uncomfortable. I respect you too much for that."

My tongue darts out to moisten my suddenly dry lips. Jasper's eyes darken as they track the movement.

"Destiny," he says again, his voice rough with an unspoken question.

And at that moment, I break. The walls I've so carefully constructed around my heart come crumbling down, the last of my resistance shattering into dust.

"Jasper," I breathe, my voice trembling with longing. "I... I want..."

But I can't finish the sentence, can't give voice to the desire pulsing through my veins.

Jasper takes another step forward, his hand coming up to cup my cheek with a tenderness that makes my eyes sting with tears.

"Tell me, sunshine," he urges softly. "Tell me what you want."

I take a shuddering breath, my heart pounding so hard I'm sure he can hear it.

"Just a taste. Just one taste, and then we can put this behind us."

Jasper's thumb strokes across my cheekbone, his touch setting my skin ablaze. "Are you sure?"

All I can think about is the feel of his hands on my skin, the hunger burning in his gaze.

"Please. Kiss me, Jasper."

Chapter 5
JASPER

TIME SEEMS TO STAND still as I gaze into Destiny's eyes, lost in the swirling depths of honey-brown. Her lips are parted, her breath coming in soft pants that send shivers down my spine.

With a trembling hand, I reach up and trace the curve of her mouth with my thumb, marveling at the softness of her skin. I've dreamed of this moment for so long, fantasized about the taste of her lips, the feel of her body pressed against mine.

Now that it's finally happening, I want to savor every second, etch every detail into my memory.

Slowly, I lower my head until our mouths are a hairsbreadth apart. I can feel the heat of her breath mingling with mine, the anticipation building in the scant space between us.

"Destiny," I murmur, my voice rough with longing. "I'm going to kiss you now."

She doesn't say a word, but the way her eyes flutter closed is all the permission I need. I close the distance between us, brushing my lips against hers in a feather-light caress.

We both sigh at the contact, a soft exhale of breath that sends tingles racing across my skin. And then I'm slanting my mouth over hers, deepening the kiss with a groan of pure need.

Destiny's hands fist in my hair as she pulls me closer. I wrap my arms around her waist, crushing her soft curves against the hard planes of my body.

Her tongue slides against mine, hot and slick and perfect, and I can't suppress the shudder that rolls through me.

My hands slip beneath the hem of her blouse, skimming over the smooth skin of her lower back. She arches into my touch, a breathy moan escaping her lips.

It's only when my fingers brush the lacy edge of her bra that I come back to my senses, the fog of lust clearing just enough for reality to come crashing back in.

I tear my mouth from hers with a gasp, my chest heaving as I struggle to catch my breath. Destiny blinks up at me, her eyes hazy with desire.

"Jasper."

I close my eyes, fighting back the urge to claim her mouth again, to lose myself in the taste of her.

"I'm sorry," she breathes, her voice trembling. "I shouldn't have... we can't..."

My eyes snap open. "I'm not sorry, Destiny."

She stares at me, her brow furrowed in confusion. "I thought a small kiss wouldn't hurt. But this isn't right. You're my boss."

"Sunshine, I haven't thought of you as just an employee for a very long time."

"What do you mean?"

I take a deep breath, knowing that the next words out of my mouth will change everything between us. But I'm done holding back, done pretending that my feelings for her are anything less than all-consuming.

"I've wanted you from the moment I first laid eyes on you,"

She flushes, her cheeks turning a becoming shade of pink. But she doesn't look away, doesn't pull out of my embrace.

"I'm not looking for a casual relationship. Taking care of Aiden is all I can manage right now."

"I don't want casual, Sunshine," I tell her, my voice fierce with conviction. "I want you in my life forever. As my wife, my life partner."

Her breath hitches, her eyes widening in shock. "Wife? Jasper, we've never even been on a date. How can you possibly know that you want to marry me?"

I brush a stray loc back from her face. "Because I know my heart, Destiny. And it belongs to you, completely."

She shakes her head, a bewildered laugh bubbling up from her throat. "This is insane. We work together, Jasper. What if things don't work out between us? I can't risk my job, my stability."

"You know me, Destiny. You know I don't make decisions lightly. When I commit to something, I'm all in."

My thumbs stroking over the soft skin of her cheeks as I take her face in my hands. "I won't let you down, Sunshine. I want to take care of you and Aiden. I want to build a life with you, to watch your belly swell with our baby."

A single tear slips down her cheek, and I catch it with my thumb. "I know it's a lot to take in. You need time to process, to think about what this means for you and Aiden."

She nods, her bottom lip caught between her teeth. "I need time to think. For Aiden's sake, as much as my own."

I kiss her forehead.

"Take all the time you need, sunshine. I'm not going anywhere."

I step back, putting some much-needed distance between us before I lose the last shreds of my self-control. Every cell in my body is screaming at me to pull her back into my arms, to show her with my hands and my mouth just how much I adore her.

But I know that's not what she needs right now. She needs space, needs time to wrap her head around the idea of us, of the future I'm offering her.

With one last long look, I force myself to turn away, to walk out of her apartment and into the cool night air. Every step feels like a physical ache, a wrenching separation from the woman who holds my heart in her hands.

As I climb into my car and turn the key in the ignition, I send up a silent prayer to whatever gods might be listening.

Please, let her choose me. Let her choose us.

Chapter 6
DESTINY

THE SOUND OF LAUGHTER and clinking glasses fills my living room as I settle onto the couch, a generous pour of red wine in hand. It's Friday night, which means it's time for our monthly girls' get-together. And this month, we're meeting at my place.

Sienna, Rosa, and Scarlett are sprawled across my furniture, their faces flushed from the wine and the easy camaraderie between us.

"I can't believe Aiden is already old enough for weekend visits with his dad," Sienna muses, sipping her wine. "Seems like just yesterday you were bringing him home from the hospital."

I smile wistfully, my heart aching a bit at the thought of my baby boy growing up so quickly. "Time flies, doesn't it? I'm just grateful that Mark is stepping up and being a more involved father. Aiden adores his grandparents, too."

"And the rest of our little monsters are happily wreaking havoc at my dad's place," Rosa chuckles. "Bless that man for being willing to take on a pack of wild children once a month."

We all raise our glasses in a toast to Rosa's saint of a father.

"Enough about the kids," Scarlett declares, a mischievous glint in her eye. "I want to hear more about Sienna's hot new man. Spill the tea, girl!"

Sienna blushes, ducking her head with a coy smile. "Things with Romeo are...intense. In the best possible way. He's so attentive and passionate, both in and out of the bedroom."

We all whoop and whistle, causing Sienna's cheeks to flame even brighter.

"Get it, girl," Rosa teases, waggling her eyebrows suggestively. "Lord knows you deserve some toe-curling orgasms after the dry spell you've had."

Sienna tosses a throw pillow at Rosa's head, giggling. "Like you're one to talk, missy. When was the last time you had a date that didn't involve chicken nuggets and a cartoon movie?"

"Touché," Rosa concedes with a grin. "But enough about my sad sex life. I want to hear what's going on with Destiny and her hot boss."

I nearly choke on my wine, my eyes widening as three pairs of curious gazes lock onto me.

"W-what do you mean?" I stammer, trying to play it cool.

Rosa rolls her eyes. "Oh, please. You've been making heart eyes at Jasper Cleveland for months now. And don't think we haven't noticed the way he looks at you when he thinks no one's watching."

"It's...complicated," I hedge, swirling my wine glass.

"Uncomplicate it for us," Scarlett urges, leaning forward eagerly. "Did something happen between you two?"

I take a deep breath, knowing there's no use trying to hide the truth from my best friends. They know me too well.

"Jasper told me he wants a serious relationship with me. That he wants forever, with me and Aiden."

A shocked silence descends over the room for a moment before it erupts in a cacophony of squeals and exclamations.

"Oh my god, Destiny!" Sienna gasps, her hand flying to her chest. "That's huge!"

"What did you say?" Scarlett demands, her eyes wide.

I shake my head, my thoughts a jumbled mess of fear and longing. "I said I needed time to think."

Rosa leans forward, her gaze intent on my face. The delicate tattoo on her collarbone, a twining vine of green leaves and red flowers, stands out in stark contrast to her caramel skin.

"How do you feel about him, Des?" she asks softly, her voice laced with understanding.

I close my eyes for a moment, letting the truth rise to the surface. "I'm in lust with him," I admit, my voice trembling slightly. "I love the way his mind works, the way he's so passionate about his job. Being around him, working with him...it's the highlight of my day. If I could have Aiden there with me, I'd never want to leave the office."

I open my eyes, meeting Rosa's sympathetic gaze. "But I'm terrified to put my trust in a man again. After what happened with Mark, the thought of getting my heart broken like that...I don't know if I could survive it a second time."

"But Jasper isn't Mark," Sienna points out. "From everything you've told us, he seems like a genuinely good guy."

I nod, worrying my bottom lip between my teeth. "He is. He's kind and smart. The way he is with Aiden...it makes my heart melt."

Scarlett giggles, the wine making her even more bubbly than usual. She's the oldest of our group and the reason we all became friends in the first place, but she's a total lightweight with alcohol.

"You two are soulmates," she declares, her words slightly slurred. "Anyone can see that you just...get each other."

"It's difficult to find a connection like that," Rosa agrees, her voice wistful.

We all go quiet for a moment. Rosa still carries a torch for her first love, the biker who got away. She rarely talks about him, but the pain of that loss still lingers in her eyes.

"Didn't you say that once Jasper makes a decision, he sticks with it no matter what?" Sienna asks, breaking the somber silence.

I remember the steely determination in Jasper's voice when he told me he wanted forever with me. "He's not the type to make impulsive choices. When he commits to something, he's all in."

Scarlett leans back against the couch cushions, her expression thoughtful. "Are you going to pass up this chance at happiness?"

My mind drifts back to last night, to the warmth and ease of having dinner with Jasper and Aiden. The way Jasper looked at my son, the tenderness in his eyes as he helped him build block towers and make silly faces...it was everything I've ever wanted for Aiden.

And the way Jasper looked at me, the heat and promise in his gaze as we sat side by side on Aiden's bed, reading him a bedtime story...it made me ache with longing for something I hadn't even realized I'd been missing.

A partner. Someone to share the joys and burdens of parenting with, someone to lean on and laugh with and love with my whole heart.

Jasper could be that for me. For Aiden.

I'm terrified, but I realize my trust in Jasper is stronger than my fear.

I set my wineglass down on the coffee table and stand up, my heart pounding in my chest.

"I need to go see him," I announce, my voice shaking with a mixture of nerves and exhilaration.

"Go get your man, girl!" Sienna crows, pumping her fist in the air.

"And don't come back until you've sealed the deal!" Scarlett adds with a wicked cackle.

Rosa stands up and pulls me into a fierce hug, her eyes shining with unshed tears. "I'm so proud of you, Destiny," she whispers. "You deserve all the love and happiness in the world."

I cling to her for a moment, drawing strength from her unwavering support. Then I'm rushing out the door, pausing only to call a taxi and grab my purse.

The ride to Cleveland Logistics seems to take an eternity, my knee bouncing with impatience as I watch the town lights blur past the window.

When we finally pull up to the gleaming glass building, my heart leaps into my throat. Most of the windows are dark, the offices empty for the night.

But there, on the top floor, a single light shines like a beacon, calling me home.

Jasper's office.

I toss a handful of bills at the driver and scramble out of the car, my heels clicking rapidly against the pavement as I hurry towards the entrance.

The elevator ride to the top floor is the longest of my life. I pace the small space, my reflection in the mirrored walls a blur of nervous energy.

When the doors finally slide open, I'm hit with a wave of déjà vu. Just last night, I was standing in this very spot, my heart in my throat as I knocked on Jasper's door.

But everything has changed since then. I've changed.

Taking a deep breath, I raise my hand and knock once; the sound echoing in the quiet hallway.

"Come in," Jasper calls, his voice sending a shiver down my spine.

I turn the knob and step inside, my gaze immediately locking with his. He's sitting behind his desk, his shirt unbuttoned at the collar and his tie nowhere to be seen. The lamplight casts his chiseled features in gold and shadow, making him look even more devastatingly handsome than usual.

"Destiny. What are you doing here? Is everything okay?"

"I'm here because...because I'm ready, Jasper."

He stands up slowly, his gaze never leaving mine. "Ready for what, Sunshine?"

I cross the room in three quick strides, coming to a stop just inches away from him. This close, I can see the flecks of green in his hazel eyes, can feel the heat of his body calling to mine.

"Ready to put my trust in you." I reach up to cup his face in my hands. I love you, Jasper Cleveland. "

His breath catches, his eyes shining with a fierce emotion. And then he's crushing me against his chest, his lips claiming mine in a kiss that feels like a promise.

Chapter 7
DESTINY

THE WORLD NARROWS DOWN to the press of jasper's lips against mine, the heat of his body seeping into my skin as he holds me close.

His hands slide down my back, his touch leaving trails of fire in their wake. I arch into him, a breathy moan escaping my lips as his fingers find the zipper of my dress.

Jasper kisses me again, his mouth hot and hungry as he walks me backwards towards his desk. I barely register the sweep of his arm, the clatter of pens and papers hitting the floor. All I can focus on is the way his body feels against mine, the hard planes and angles that make me ache to be even closer.

He tugs the dress zipper down with a deliberate slowness that makes me shiver. I let the fabric slide off my shoulders, pooling at my feet in a whisper of silk.

He breaks the kiss to look at me, his gaze scorching as it rakes over my body. I'm wearing a simple black bra and panty set, nothing fancy or overtly seductive. But the way Jasper is looking at me, makes me feel precious.

"You're so beautiful," he rasps, his hands coming up to cup my breasts through the thin fabric of my bra. "I've dreamed about this moment, about seeing you like this.

I flush, warmth blooming in my chest at his words. No one has ever made me feel as desired, as cherished, as Jasper does.

"I want to see you too," I whisper, my fingers fumbling with the buttons of his shirt.

He helps me, shrugging out of the garment and tossing it aside. My breath catches at the sight of his bare chest, the defined muscles and golden skin that make my fingers itch to touch.

"Like what you see?" he teases, his eyes glinting with mischief.

I nod, biting my lip as I reach out to run my hands over his shoulders, his arms, his chest. "Very much so," I murmur, my voice husky with want.

Jasper groans, his head falling back as my fingers explore the ridges and planes of his torso. "You're killing me, Sunshine," he growls, his hands flexing on my hips.

I grin, emboldened by his reaction to my touch. Slowly, tantalizingly, I drag my nails down his abdomen, feeling the muscles jump and quiver beneath his skin.

When I reach the waistband of his slacks, I pause, looking up at him through my lashes. "Can I?" I ask softly, my fingers toying with the button.

"Please," he grits out, his eyes nearly black with desire.

I pop the button free and slide down the zipper, my hand brushing against the hard length of him as I push the fabric off his hips. He kicks the slacks away, leaving him in just a pair of black boxer briefs.

I swallow hard, sudden nerves fluttering in my stomach. It's been so long since I've been with a man, and never with someone I cared about as deeply as I do Jasper.

As if sensing my hesitation, Jasper cups my face in his hands, his thumbs stroking over my cheekbones. "We can take this as slow as you need, Destiny," he murmurs, his eyes soft with understanding. "I'm not going anywhere."

I shake my head, pressing a kiss to his palm. "I don't want to go slow," I admit, my voice barely above a whisper. "I want you, Jasper. All of you. Tonight."

His eyes flare with heat. "Then you'll have me," he promises, his voice rough with emotion.

Tears prick at the backs of my eyes, the depth of his love stealing my breath. "I'm yours too," I whisper, my heart in my throat.

Jasper kisses me, a deep, drugging kiss that makes my toes curl and my blood sing. His hands roam over my body, leaving trails of fire in their wake as he unhooks my bra and slides my panties down my legs.

I step out of them, kicking them aside as Jasper lifts me onto the edge of his desk. The wood is cool against my bare skin, a delicious contrast to the heat of his body as he settles between my thighs.

"I love you, Destiny!" he breathes, his lips trailing down the column of my throat.

"I love you too," I gasp, my head falling back as he takes one of my nipples into his mouth. "Oh God, Jasper..."

He lavishes attention on my breasts, his lips and tongue and teeth driving me to the brink of madness. I'm panting, my hips rocking against his in a desperate search for friction, for relief from the ache building inside me.

Jasper slides one hand down my stomach, his fingers dipping into the slick heat between my thighs. I cry out, my nails digging into his shoulders as he strokes me with a knowing touch, circling my clit until I'm writhing beneath him.

"That's it, baby," he murmurs, his voice a low rumble against my skin. "Let go for me. I've got you."

I shatter in his arms, my body convulsing with the force of my release. Jasper holds me through it, whispering words of love and praise as I come down from the high.

When I finally catch my breath, I open my eyes to find him watching me with a look of such tenderness, it makes my heart clench.

"I need you," I whisper, my hands sliding down his back to the waistband of his boxer briefs. "Please, Jasper."

Together, we rid him of the last barrier between us, baring him to my hungry gaze.

I lick my lips, my mouth going dry at the sight of him, hard and ready and absolutely perfect. I've never wanted anyone the way I want Jasper in this moment, with a desperation that borders on pain.

Jasper positions himself at my entrance, the blunt head of his cock nudging against my sensitive flesh.

"Look at me, Sunshine," he commands softly, waiting until my eyes meet his. "I'm going to take care of you, always. You're safe with me."

Tears burn in my eyes at the fierce sincerity in his voice. I frame his face with my hands. "I trust you, Jasper."

He kisses me then pushes forward, slowly, carefully, filling me inch by exquisite inch until he's buried to the hilt.

We both groan. Jasper stills, giving me a moment to adjust to the stretch, the fullness.

He presses his forehead against mine. "I'll never let anyone hurt you again, Destiny."

I'm too overwhelmed for words. Because I know, bone deep, that with his strong hands and steady heart, Jasper will be my home.

He begins to move then, slowly at first, his hips rocking against mine in a steady rhythm. I wrap my legs around his waist, urging him deeper, needing to feel every inch of him inside me.

Jasper growls, his thrusts becoming harder, more urgent. The desk creaks beneath us, the sound mingling with our pants and moans, the slap of skin against skin.

"So tight," he grits out, his face buried in the crook of my neck. "So perfect. God, Destiny, you feel incredible."

"So do you," I gasp, my head thrown back in ecstasy. "Don't stop, Jasper. Please don't stop."

He doesn't. He drives into me again and again, hitting that spot inside me that makes stars explode behind my eyelids. I cling to him, my nails raking down his back as the pressure builds inside me, coiling tighter and tighter until I'm sure I'll break from the force of it.

"Let go," Jasper rasps, his hand sliding between our bodies to rub my clit. "Come for me, Sunshine. I want to feel you."

And just like that, I'm flying apart, my body shattering into smithereens. I cry out his name, my voice hoarse and broken as wave after wave of pleasure crashes over me.

Jasper follows me over the edge with a shout, his hips jerking erratically as he spills himself inside me. I feel the hot rush of his release, the pulsing of his cock as he empties himself into my willing body.

We cling to each other, our chests heaving and our skin slick with sweat. Jasper peppers my face with kisses, whispering sweet nothings against my flushed skin.

And in that moment, I know I've made the right choice.

Epilogue

JASPER

One Year later

THE SUN IS SHINING bright in the clear blue sky, a perfect day for our wedding. I stand at the altar, my heart racing with anticipation as I watch the guests take their seats on the lush lawn of the Cleveland mansion.

It's been a year since Destiny trusted me and changed my life forever. A year of laughter, love, and happiness I never knew existed. And today, in front of our family and friends, we're making it official.

"You ready for this, big brother?" My younger brother, Ethan, claps me on the shoulder, a wide grin splitting his face.

"I've never been more ready for anything in my life."

And it's true. From the moment I met Destiny, I knew she was the woman I wanted to build a life and a family with.

I scan the crowd, my heart swelling at the sight of so many loved ones gathered to celebrate our special day.

IRIS WEST

My mom is sitting in the front row, her eyes already misty with tears of joy. Beside her is my grandmother, looking regal and proud in her pale blue dress suit.

Behind them are my cousins and uncles, a rowdy bunch who have been teasing me mercilessly about finally settling down. But beneath the jokes and jabs, I can see the genuine happiness in their eyes, the love and support that has always been the backbone of the Cleveland clan.

And then there's Destiny's family, a sea of dress uniforms and bright smiles. Her father, a colonel, cuts an imposing figure in his decorated blues. Her mother is a vision in a vibrant floral dress, the brightest frock I've ever seen. It suits her personality perfectly, warm and effervescent and full of life.

Destiny's siblings are here too - her older sister and her military husband, her two brothers who followed in their father's footsteps, and her younger sister who's practically vibrating with excitement. So are her best friends - Sienna, Rosa, and Scarlett - their faces glowing with happiness for their beloved friend.

But it's the sight of Aiden, our ring bearer, that makes my breath catch in my throat. He's walking down the aisle with a solemn determination that belies his tender age, the pillow with our rings clutched tightly in his small hands.

He's grown so much in the last year, not just physically but emotionally too. He's opened his heart to me in a way that humbles me, accepting me not just as his mother's partner but as a second dad.

As he reaches the altar, he looks up at me with a toothy grin, his eyes sparkling with mischief and love. "I did good, daddy?" he whispers, his voice carrying in the hushed silence.

I swallow hard, blinking back the sudden sting of tears. "You did perfect, buddy," I whisper back, ruffling his hair.

And then the music swells and everyone rises to their feet.

Destiny appears at the end of the aisle, a vision in white lace and tulle. Her dress is simple and elegant, hugging her curves in all the right places before flaring out into a graceful train.

But it's the look on her face that steals my breath, the radiant joy and love that seems to light her from within. She's always been beautiful to me, but today, she's transcendent.

Her father walks her down the aisle, his arm linked with hers. I can see the emotion welling in his eyes, the bittersweet mix of pride and sadness that every father feels on his daughter's wedding day.

When they reach me, he places Destiny's hand in mine, his grip firm. "Take care of my baby girl, son," he says gruffly.

"Always," I vow, my eyes never leaving Destiny's.

He takes his seat beside his wife, who's already dabbing at her eyes with a lace handkerchief.

And then it's just us, standing hand in hand before the officiant, ready to pledge our lives and our love to each other.

The ceremony passes in a blur of laughter and tears, of heartfelt vows and shaky "I dos." When the officiant pronounces us husband and wife, I sweep Destiny into my arms and kiss her with all the love and passion in my heart.

The crowd erupts into cheers and applause, but I barely hear them. All I can focus on is the woman in my arms, the woman who has become my universe.

"I love you," I murmur against her lips, my voice rough with emotion.

"I love you too," she whispers back, her eyes shining with happy tears. "Forever and always."

"Forever and always," I echo, sealing the promise with another kiss.

We turn to face our family and friends, hand in hand, ready to begin our new life together.

The reception is a whirlwind of music and dancing, of toasts and laughter and more food than I've ever seen in my life.

Mom and Granny hug Destiny.

"You take good care of my grandson, you hear?" Mom says mock-sternly, her eyes twinkling with mirth.

Destiny laughs, hugging her tightly. "I'll do my best, but something tells me he's going to be spoiled rotten by his Cleveland grandmas."

"Damn straight," Granny chimes in, her voice filled with affection. "That boy is going to be loved within an inch of his life."

I catch Destiny's eye over their heads, my heart swelling with love and gratitude. This woman, this incredible woman, has not only given me her heart but has opened her family to me, to us.

Throughout the night, I watch as she dances with her father, her brothers, her friends. Her laughter rings out across the lawn, a joyful sound that I know I'll never tire of hearing.

And when it's time for our first dance as husband and wife, I take her in my arms and hold her close, swaying to the music as the rest of the world falls away.

"How did I get so lucky?" My lips brush against her temple.

"I ask myself the same thing every day."

"Thank you," I say suddenly, my throat tight with emotion.

She tilts her head, curiosity flickering in her gaze. "For what?"

"For taking a chance on me."

Her eyes fill with tears, her hand coming up to cup my cheek. "Jasper, you are my family. You and Aiden, you're my entire world. I'm the one who should thank you for showing me what real love looks like."

I lean down and capture her lips in a soft, sweet kiss. "I'll spend the rest of my life showing you," I promise. "Every day, for the rest of our lives."

She smiles against my mouth, her arms tightening around my neck. "I'm going to hold you to that, Mr. Cleveland."

"I'm counting on it, Mrs. Cleveland."

We dance until the stars come out, until the guests trickle away and the band packs up for the night.

And then it's just us, walking hand in hand across the moonlit lawn, Aiden fast asleep in my arms.

"Ready to start our forever?" I ask, my heart so full it feels like it might burst.

Destiny leans her head against my shoulder, her fingers lacing with mine. "I've never been more ready for anything in my life."

And as we make our way back to the house, to the life we've built together, I know that this is just the beginning of a love story that will last a lifetime.

SINGLE MOM AND THE BIKER

BLOSSOM FORD MOMS BOOK 3

IRIS WEST

Chapter 1
ROSA

I HUM AS I expertly roll out the flaky dough for my famous buttermilk pies. The sweet, rich scent of butter and sugar fills the small kitchen of Rosa's Treats, the bakery I took over four years ago. When I was in elementary school, I used to come in just to smell the bread, cakes and pastries. Then, it was Kendy's Bakery.

After I turned fifteen, I pestered Miss. Delores, the sweet, old lady who used to own it, to let me work after school and on Saturdays. I became a full-time employee as soon as I graduated high school, twelve years ago. It was my dream to spend my days creating delicious pastries and cakes to brighten people's lives, the way my mama's buttermilk pie used to brighten my days. Seeing the smiles on my customers' faces makes all the early mornings and sore feet worth it.

The bell above the door tinkles and I glance up to see my beautiful, eleven-year-old twin girls spill inside, their matching ponytails bouncing and faces glowing with excitement. My heart swells. Giving birth to and raising Tatiana and Tamara is the best decision I ever made in my life.

"Mama!" they call out, rushing around the counter to hug me tight. I laugh and squeeze them back.

My friend Scarlet's daughter trails in behind the twins. Clem had a successful bone marrow transplant a year ago to cure leukemia and each day she grows stronger.

"Hi Tía Rosa," Clem says.

I hug her.

"We came say goodbye. Abuelo Carlos has all the camping gear stacked in the back of his pickup truck," she says.

I pull back and eye Tatiana and Tamara sternly, hands on my hips. "You better behave for my papa, you hear? No crazy stunts like last summer! Poor Abuelo nearly had a heart attack when you decided to 'explore' that cave."

"We promise, Mama," the twins chorus, giving me their best innocent looks. I narrow my eyes but can't stop my lips from twitching. They are too adorable for their own good.

"Uh huh. I'm counting on you to keep these two troublemakers in line, Clem."

"You got it, Tía." Clem salute, like her daddy was. "I'll make sure they stick to the trails and don't harass the wildlife."

We all laugh at that, knowing my animal-loving girls are more likely to try and adopt every cute creature they come across. Including the baby skunk they found last year.

Shaking my head, I shoo them out from behind the counter. "Alright you three, get going before Abuelo changes his mind about taking you at all!

The girls all hug me one more time, before scampering out the door and heading towards home, which is only a couple of minutes away.

I get back to my baking, grateful I'll have a whole weekend of peace. This summer break has been crazy busy so I'm glad the twins return to school next week. As I crimp the edges of the piecrust, my mind drifts. What would it be like to have a partner to share all this with? Someone to be a father figure for the girls, a companion for me.

I shake off the wistful thoughts with a sigh. I'm lucky to have such an incredible support system with my dad and best friends. Scarlett, Destiny, and Sienna have been my rocks over the years, helping me juggle work and motherhood as fellow single moms. I don't know what I'd do without their friendship.

The growl of a motorcycle pulling up outside jerks me out of my little pity party. I glance out the front window, expecting to see one of the local bikers who occasionally stop in for a slice of pie and cup of coffee.

My heart nearly leaps out of my chest when I recognize the rider. Even with his back to me, I would know those broad shoulders and midnight hair anywhere. That black leather jacket hugging his muscular frame, those long legs straddling the powerful machine between them and the way he sits on the motorcycle.

Raidon.

He swings off the bike in one smooth move, all coiled strength and predatory grace. Razor-sharp cheekbones and piercing gray eyes flash in my mind, memories of the past threatening to swamp me. I grip the edge of the counter, my knees suddenly wobbly.

What is he doing here? After twelve years of silence he shows up at my shop out of the blue? Anger flares in my chest but it can't overpower the wild fluttering beneath my ribs. Damn him. Still as devastatingly sexy as ever, with gorgeous tattoos and a devil may care swagger. He stalks toward the bakery door like he owns the place, gaze on me.

The tinkling of the bell is a jarring cheerful sound in the electrically charged moment. And then he's here, standing in front of me, all six feet plus of hard, dangerous male. I'm pinned in place by his glacial eyes, my tongue suddenly cleaved to the roof of my mouth. I want to rail at him, cuss him up one side and down the other, demand to know where the hell he's been all this time.

But I don't. Not with the way he's looking at me, as if he's spied an oasis after days without water and the memories of our one passionate evening together still seared into my brain. He's the only man I've ever been with. The father of my kids.

"Hello, Rosebud." I nearly whimper at the sound of that low, gravelly purr. His eyes rake my short body from head to toe and I feel branded by his gaze, heat trickling down my spine. "Been a while."

"Raidon," I manage through stiff lips, my fingers curling into my palms. Be strong, Rosa. Don't let him sweep you of your feet. "What are you doing here?"

One dark brow lifts and a wistful smile tugs at the corner of that sensual mouth. "I missed you. So much. And this scent." He sniffs the air. "I've been dreaming of your sweet treats ever since I left."

I feel my face flush, the double meaning in his words wrapping around me like a velvet caress. I want to lean into his heat, breathe in the scent of leather and warm male skin.

I can't do this. I have my girls to think about. I will not let myself get involved with a man who blows in and out of my life on a whim. Any heartbreak I suffer will affect them too. They deserve so much better than that.

Squaring my shoulders, I lift my chin, desperately trying to gather the threads of my composure. "The pies aren't ready yet. If that's all you came for, I'm afraid you'll have to come back later."

"That isn't all I came for."

His eyes are dark, desire and something that appears to be longing swirling in them. Why does every word he say seem like the truth? I don't understand why I feel compelled to trust

Raidon, why my soul decided he's a good guy. If he truly longed for me, he'd have returned to Blossom Ford over a decade ago. He probably just wants a pussy to grind into.

He steps closer, crowding me back against the counter. The heat of him washes over me, his presence overwhelming in the small space.

"Can we talk? I owe you an explanation."

His face is just inches from mine now and I can't tear my eyes away from his mouth. Heart pounding, I scramble for the tattered shreds of my anger. My hurt. But under the searing spotlight of his gaze, it's all too easy to remember how those firm lips felt on my fevered skin, those calloused fingers skating over my curves. I shiver, fighting the urge to arch into him like a cat.

Chapter 2

RAIDON

ROSA STILL HAS THE same effect on me as she did twelve years ago. I can't take my eyes off her curvier body. My cock stiffens at the flush on her cheeks and the way her rosy lips part slightly, as if inviting me in. My hands itch to bring her body flush against mine, to feel her round tits and wide hips pressed against my hard body.

Everything in me screams fucking mine, like it did twelve years ago. It takes every ounce of the discipline I practiced over the last decade to prevent myself from, throwing her over my shoulder, depositing her on my bike and taking her into the mountains to fuck her until she's screaming with pleasure and crying out my name.

The bakery still smells of doughnuts and buttermilk pie, the spicy-sweet aroma that first drew me in all those years ago when I laid eyes on Rosa. That scent became my salvation, the memory I clung to during the darkest days of the eleven years I spent in prison. When the stench and despair threatened to overwhelm me, I'd close my eyes and imagine that sugary fragrance enveloping me, transporting me back to that perfect evening with Rosa.

I was a gruff, jaded, twenty-six-year-old fucker, with a chip on my shoulder, whose only salvation was the fourteen-year-old sister I raised. Despite the multiple rings on her ears, the tattoo on her belly of her mom's favorite pie and the sinful curves on her body, Rosa was all innocence with a giving spirit that stole my heart. In the couple of hours we spent together after her shift ended, I learned of her dream to be a baker, how she loved her hometown and never wanted to leave, and the happy childhood she'd had before her mom passed away.

Since my release a year ago, my body has been yearning for her with a ferocity that sometimes robs me of breath. The only relief I could find was when I took myself in hand, fisting my cock with her name on my lips as I imagined sinking into her lush warmth.

I deserve every ounce of the anger and suspicion I see in those honey eyes. Hell, I'm lucky she didn't toss my ass out on the sidewalk the second she recognized me.

The fact she's not wearing a ring fills me with immense satisfaction. She's the kind of woman who'd wear a ring if she were married. Just like I would, so everyone would know I was taken.

"I don't think so," she says through gritted teeth, sliding out from between me and the counter and putting a few feet of distance between us. "I have work to do. If you're not going to buy anything, I'll have to ask you to leave."

I feel my jaw clench, frustration at myself for not being able to explain better humming through my veins. I assess the stubborn set of her lush mouth, the wary distrust in the tight line of her shoulders. Pushing her now will only make her dig her heels in deeper. As much as it kills me, I need to back off. Give her time.

"I can take a hint. I'll get out of your hair." I turn for the door, already feeling the loss of her warmth, her scent, her mere presence after so long without. But I'm not giving up. I look back over my shoulder, pinning her with a heated gaze full of promise. "I'll be seeing you, Rosebud."

I'm reaching for the door handle when it suddenly flies open and two missiles burst into the bakery.

"Mama! Tamara forgot her--"

The rest of the words fade into background noise as I stare at the girls, taller than Rosa, my brain struggling to process what I'm seeing. They're identical, from the waves of glossy brown-black hair to the smooth peach skin and the familiar slightly uptilted gray eyes currently widening as they catch sight of me. But it's the tiny dark mole just to the left of both their noses that has all the air whooshing out of my lungs in a stunned rush.

I know that birthmark. I've seen it every day of my life, on my sorry excuse of a father, on me and later on my kid sister Storm.

These girls can't be more than eleven or twelve and they look exactly the way Storm did when she was their age.

If they are what the calculating part of my brain is insisting they must be, if their age matches up with that evening when I took Rosa's virginity, then I'm a father. Holy shit.

What did Rosa go through? My heart hurts at the shock she must have suffered when she found out she was pregnant. I used a condom to protect her.

How did she cope with bringing two babies into the world when she was only eighteen?

The room tilts around me. Roaring fills my ears. I look at Rosa, really look at her, taking in the sudden pallor under her caramel skin, the stricken, almost fearful expression on her face as she stares back at me. And I know.

They're my little girls.

I open my mouth, not even sure what I'm going to say, my whole world upended in the space of a few seconds. But Rosa is already moving, putting herself between me and the twins - Christ, my daughters - a fierce, protective mama bear.

I thought you were leaving with Abuelo. Mija, what did you forget?" Her voice is overly bright, thin with strain.

The one who spoke first bites her lip, obviously picking up on the sudden tension. "Tamara forgot her ping mosquito repellant bracelet when we helped you yesterday," she says, her eyes darting between me and Rosa.

Chapter 3
RAIDON

ROSA USHERS THE GIRLS toward the back of the kitchen. It feels like a dismissal. They disappear from my view for a moment then the girls rush back out, giving me one last curious look.

I stumble toward the mother of my kids. "Rosa, are they, I mean, fuck." Eloquent as always, Douglas, I snicker silently. I stole myself for the fact my woman might be happy with another man, even though I desperately hoped she was single. I wanted to make sure she was okay. For her, I would have walked away if she were happy, even if it killed me.

Being a dad never crossed my mind.

Rosa whips around to face me, her dark eyes flashing with a maelstrom of emotions. "No," she says, low and fierce.

No, they aren't mine? No, I can't ask questions? Or, I don't have the right.

"Rosebud."

IRIS WEST

My voice is wrecked. So much for the tough, stoic biker image. But I can't muster up any shame over it. "Please. Just tell me their names at least."

She stares me down for a long, charged moment. I watch the war play out across her expressive face--anger, fear, defiance, sorrow. I put all of that there and the knowledge sits like a stone in my gut. Finally, her rigid shoulders droop in defeat.

"Tatiana and Tamara," she says, her voice barely above a whisper. "They're eleven."

Her words are hammer blows to my solar plexus. I feel the impact of those missing years like a physical thing, the weight of all the milestones and memories I wasn't part of. First steps, first words, first days of school, all of it gone.

I'm reaching for Rosa before I even realize I've moved. Her whole body goes rigid and she throws up a hand as if to hold me off. "No," she says again, shaking her head. "You don't get to do this. You don't get to just show up out of nowhere and turn our lives upside down on a whim. I won't do that to my girls."

"I know," I rasp, holding her gaze intently, willing her to see my sincerity. "I fucked up. A father shouldn't hurt his kids or their mother. But you have to let me explain, Rosa. Let me tell you why I left, why it's taken me so goddamn long to make my way back to you."

I take a cautious step closer, encouraged when she doesn't immediately retreat. "When I said you were mine while I loved you, I meant it. I was yours too. I was going to convince you to marry me and was ready to move here with my kid sister."

"We can't do this here." She casts a furtive glance toward the front of the bakery. "We could be interrupted any minute. Come back tonight, after I close up."

I leave the bakery on wooden legs, my head so full of noise it's a wonder I can even see straight. I swing a leg over my bike on autopilot, the rumble of the engine the only thing tethering me to reality as I point the front wheel toward the hills.

Part of me itches to pull out my phone and call Tech, have him run a deep background check on Rosa, soak up every scrap of information on the last eleven years of her life that I can get my hands on. But I shove the impulse down. That would be wrong. I must hear it from her.

Almost before I realize it, I'm pulling up in front of the sprawling new compound that houses the Devil's Mountain MC. My brothers. My chosen family. I know they'll have a million questions, be chomping at the bit for details on why I tore out of here like the hounds of hell were on my heels.

But I'm not ready to share this with them yet. It's too new, too raw. An exposed nerve. I need to process on my own before I can even begin to talk it through with anyone else, if I ever do that.

I'm the resident loner of the club and they're used to me going silent for stretches. No one will think much of me squirreling myself away for a few hours.

IRIS WEST

I head for the garage, burying myself elbow-deep in the guts of the '69 Triumph I've been restoring. The familiar bite of grease and metal grounds me, forces my chaotic thoughts into some semblance of order as my hands work independent of my mind.

But even that age-old routine can't stop the images playing on a loop behind my eyes. Rosa, her belly swollen with my children. The twins as chubby toddlers, taking their first stumbling steps. Missing teeth smiles on the first day of kindergarten. Eleven years of birthdays and Christmases scraped knees and school plays. All the moments I should have been there for and wasn't.

Growing up, I didn't know these moments were special. I barely attended school. My biological mother took off when I was three. My father was too busy finding his next alcohol fix to take me to school. As I grew, he took to using me as a punch bag, so more often than not, I was too embarrassed to go in with bruises or was in too much pain. However, when Storm was born, I made sure she went to school, I was there for all her firsts and school plays. I know how much I've missed by not being in my daughters' lives.

Chapter 4

ROSA

I STARE AT THE door long after Raidon's broad shoulders have disappeared through it, my heart beating a wild tattoo against my ribs.

I try to focus my attention on the half-finished buttermilk pies waiting on the counter. But it's no use. My mind is a riot of memories and emotions, all tangled up in piercing gray eyes and the low rumble of that achingly familiar voice.

Raidon. Just his name makes me shiver and ache in places I'd long thought dormant.

How is it possible that he still has this effect on me? That one smoldering look from him can reduce me to a quivering mess, like no time has passed at all.

I stumble through the rest of my baking in a daze, my hands working on autopilot as my thoughts churn and spiral. It's a small miracle I don't burn anything, my mind a million miles from the mixing bowls and pie tins.

IRIS WEST

The moment Melany, my shop assistant, arrives I'm out the door. I mumble some vague excuse about not feeling well, ignoring the concern in her young eyes. I need to think and breathe air that isn't thick with the scent of sugar, spice and Raidon's cologne.

A few moments later, I enter the cheerful home I grew up in.

"Hi, Mom," I whisper as I pass the large, framed photo of her in the front hallway. I trail my fingers over the glass, my throat tightening with a familiar pang of longing.

It's been sixteen years since cancer stole her from us, but sometimes the loss still hits me hard. Especially on days like today, when my heart feels raw and exposed, desperate for her warm type of comfort.

What would she say if she could see me now? If she knew the father of her beloved granddaughters had suddenly reappeared, turning our carefully ordered world upside down with a few heated words and scorching glances?

I climb the stairs to my bedroom, each leaden step. I strip off my flour-dusted clothes and step into the shower, groaning as the hot spray pounds down on my tight shoulders.

Unbidden, my mind flashes to another time I was naked and wet, strong hands gliding over my slick skin as a gravelly voice rumbled filthy praise in my ear.

A pulse of heat throbs between my thighs and I gasp, my nipples tightening into aching peaks. Oh god, I'm turned on.

Achingly aroused in a way I haven't been in longer than I care to admit.

When was the last time I even thought about sex? About pleasure and passion and the slick glide of skin on skin?

Somehow, in the chaos of single motherhood and building my business and just trying to survive, that part of me had withered. When the girls were older and I tried to date, I couldn't relate to any of the men my friends tried to set me up with. I convinced myself that my libido had dried up.

What a joke. Apparently all it takes is one scorching look from Raidon and my body is ready to beg for it.

I shudder, torn between disgust and relief. It should scare me, the way he can affect me so viscerally after all this time. The way he can set me on fire with nothing more than a rumbled word and a flash of dark sky eyes.

But instead, I feel alive in a way I haven't been in years.

It terrifies me and thrills me in equal measure.

Confused and frustrated, I turn the water to icy cold, hissing as it hits my overheated flesh. I refuse to touch myself. Refuse to indulge the ache he's stirred to life so effortlessly.

I won't give him that power over me. Not again. Not when I don't know if I can survive the fallout a second time.

Shivering, I shut off the water and step out, roughly toweling myself dry. I'm just tugging a clean sundress over my head when my cell phone rings.

"Hey, honey." The warm, rich tones of Scarlett's voice wash over me when I answer the phone. "You got a minute?"

I sink onto my bed, rubbing a hand over my face. "Yeah, of course. What's up?"

"Oh, nothing much. Just checking in." There's a studied casualness to her words that makes me instantly suspicious. "Clem mentioned you seemed a little off when they popped in to pick up Tamara's bracelet. Thought maybe you could use a friendly ear."

I didn't even see her. She must have been waiting for Tatiana and Tamara outside. "Clem is thirteen going on thirty, I swear." I smile because I love how caring the teenager is despite all she's gone through.

Scarlett chuckles, the sound a hug. "She's an old soul, that one. Notices more than she ought to." A beat. "So. You want to tell me what's got you twisting up those pretty panties of yours?"

And just like that, I'm spilling everything. Raidon's sudden reappearance. His shocking discovery of his relationship to the girls. His insistence on being a part of our lives, that I'm the only woman for him.

I'm so conflicted. A part of me wants to believe him. But I'm terrified of what it will do to the girls if I let him in and he decides he can't hack it."

"Oh, honey. It's scary."

"Still, forget about the girls for a minute. I know!" She cuts off my instinctive protest. "They're the center of your world. As they should be. But first, focus on what your heart wants you to do."

I press my lips together, my throat hot and tight. "I still love him, Scar. God help me, after everything, I'm still crazy stupid in love with him."

"I know you are. And that's huge. That kind of love doesn't come around every day."

"What are you saying?"

"You trusted that man enough to give him your heart and your body."

She pauses, letting that sink in. "Maybe you owe it to yourself to genuinely hear him out. Maybe something did happen, and he couldn't return. Remember what you said moons ago when you told us about him? You were sure something tragic happened from the way he reacted during and after the phone call."

"And the girls? What do I tell them? How do I explain?"

"The truth, honey. Cross that bridge when and if you come to it. Besides, in my experience whatever puts a light in Mama's eyes usually makes her babies happy."

"How'd you get to be so wise, Scar?"

She just laughs.

We talk for a few minutes more. By the time we say our goodbyes, the anxious roil in my gut has settled to a bearable simmer.

I'm still scared, but I'm hoping Raidon has a damn good reason for only coming back now.

Chapter 5
RAIDON

I PICK UP ROSA outside the bakery. She's striking in a pair of blue jeans that hugs her curvy hips and ass and is wearing high-heeled boots. I remember her height was the single thing about herself she said she'd change if she could.

I fix a helmet on her head and she hops on behind me. The sensation of her hands on my waist and her thighs pressed against mine is heaven. We ride to a café outside of town and I grab us coffee.

I scrub a hand over my face, trying to organize the chaos in my head into some kind of cohesive narrative.

"The call I received that evening was from my sister Storm. She could barely talk. The only things I understood were blood down there and hurt. I knew something was terribly wrong. All I could think about was getting to her. I raised her from when she turned five. Making sure she was safe was my responsibility."

The old rage coils in my gut like a snake, the fury and helpless guilt as potent now as it was that day. "She was fourteen fucking years old and an asshole raped her, Rosa. She'd screamed so much, she couldn't talk. because the bastard's daddy was some hot shot politician, the cops didn't do a damned thing about it. Swept it right under the rug."

I swallow hard against the bitter taste in my mouth. Rosa makes a soft sound, her eyes wide with horror and dawning comprehension.

"Storm was so broken and scared and hurting in ways no teenage girl should ever have to hurt. I had to get justice for my sister when no one else would."

My hands fist on the table. Rosa wraps her hands around mine.

"I found someone to care for Storm then tracked him down. I wanted him to feel pain and humiliation the way Storm had. I beat him until he was in pain and bleeding, then called an ambulance and the cops."

I hear Rosa's sharp intake of breath but I don't look at her. I can't. If I see condemnation or disgust in her eyes, I don't think I can get the rest of this out.

"I went to prison for assault. A few days later, the bastard died of a heart attack and I was charged with murder."

Rosa's hands tighten.

"While awaiting trial, I met Bear, the president of the Devil's Mountain MC and did him a favor. His brothers worked on my case and found the hidden evidence that showed my beating didn't directly cause the heart attack. Instead of murder, they got me a manslaughter conviction. I served eleven years.

Slowly, I lift my eyes to Rosa's, terrified of what I'll find. What I see steals the breath from my lungs. Tears course down her face unchecked. But there's no revulsion in that watery gaze. Only terrible sadness and understanding.

"Oh, Raidon." It's only a broken whisper, but it's enough to have me crossing the space between us in two long strides, my arms aching to fold her close, to shield her from the harsh ugliness of my reality. She comes willingly, her face fitting into the hollow of my neck like she was made to be there.

"I would've waited for you." The words are muffled against my throat. I thought you changed your mind and didn't want me after all."

"Never." I cradle her head in my palm, pressing my lips to her temple. She's so small in my arms, so soft. So strong. "You're the only woman I ever wanted, Rosebud. Then and now. Prison was hell on earth most days. But you and the memory of our sweet time together got me through. The fact that a sweet thing like you gave her heart to me was a gift I treasured when the guilt of failing to protect Storm and the sick words my father used to throw at me threatened to make me believe I was a worthless piece of shit.

"It wasn't you who let her down, Rai. You raised and loved her. I'm sure she knew that. If she's anything like me, she was probably glad she had someone in her corner even though she missed you and probably felt bad you missed out on so much of your life."

"Can you forgive me and give me a chance to be a good partner and dad? I'm moving to Blossom Ford and have a steady job repairing motorcycles and restoring vintage bikes."

Rosa pulls away and looks into my eyes. "Let's take it slow. The girls will need time to adjust."

"That's good enough for me," I say, humbled and full of gratitude.

"Would you like to have dinner at my place tomorrow night?"

"Yes!" I'm not giving her time to take back her words.

Chapter 6

ROSA

I PACE THE LIVING room, my stomach a knot of nerves as I glance at the clock for the hundredth time. It's 6:05pm. Raidon is five minutes late.

I strain my ears, listening for the distinctive rumble of his motorcycle.

Ten more minutes crawl by with agonizing slowness. Still no Raidon. No call. No text. Nothing.

A sick, sinking feeling takes root in my gut. I know something must have happened. I trust him but I can't stop the anxiety spreading through me.

After another five minutes, I have to hold back from calling myself a naïve fool. Tears sting my eyes, but I blink them back. I want Raidon to come so badly and prove that I was right to place my trust in him that I realize how much I still love him.

My cell rings. I lunge for it, knocking over a stack of magazines in my haste.

Raidon's name flashes on the screen.

"Hello?"

"Rosa, there was an accident on the mountain. A hiker fell and was unconscious. I was on the phone with paramedics so haven't been able to call. The ambulance just got here. I'll be there in ten minutes."

"Is he okay?"

It's sad that hearing about the accident melted away my anxiety and made me giddy with relief.

"Hopefully, he'll be." Raidon exhales heavily and I can picture him scrubbing a hand over his stubbled jaw. "I'm on my way. Okay?"

"Okay." It comes out smaller than I intend. I turn my face away from the phone like that could hide the naked emotion in my voice. "I'll see you in a bit."

The line goes dead, and I sink into the couch.

Seven minutes later, the rumble of his bike finally shatters the silence in the house.

I yank the door open just as he bounds up the porch steps, an apology tumbling from his lips.

"I'm so sorry."

The open, earnest regret on his face squeezes my heart.

"I hate that we're getting off to a bad start. I will spend every day for the rest of my life showing you and our girls what a steady, dependable man I can be."

Our girls. It spills out of him so naturally, I want to cry and laugh at the same time.

"I started to worry. I guess it'll take some time before you being late without notice stops worrying me."

He kisses my forehead.

I blink, touched. "The lasagna should be cooled off enough to eat."

"I'm starving. For food and anything else you want to throw my way."

I roll my eyes, biting the inside of my cheek to keep from grinning like a silly girl.

Raidon tucks into the cheesy lasagna and grunts his appreciation. We talk about his work and his new home with the Devil's Mountain MC.

When we're done, he insists on washing up. I sit and watch the muscles on his back and ass flex.

We settle on the couch with ice-cold beers, Raidon's eyes land on the stack of photo albums on the end table.

"Are those pictures of the girls?"

My heart clenches at the raw need in his voice. The almost reverent way he reaches for the top album, his fingers skating over the embossed lettering. 'Tatiana and Tamara, Ages 0-2'.

"Yeah,"

He flips open the cover with shaking hands and I watch his face as he takes in the first glossy photo. The twins, only minutes old. Red faced and squalling in my arms as I beamed exhaustedly at the camera from my hospital bed.

"They're so tiny. You're glowing, Rosa. You gave birth to them all on your own."

"I wasn't alone," I rasp. "I had my dad. And later, my friends. They're all the family."

"I'm so fucking sorry I wasn't here with you."

I have to look away, the regret on his face too much to bear. "Me too."

As he flips through the album, I watch the emotions chase themselves over his rugged features - awe, pride, grief, longing. He pauses on a picture of the twins on their first birthday, faces smeared with pink frosting as they grin gummily at the camera.

"Tell me about this?" His voice is a gravelly rasp, knuckles white where he grips the album. "I want to know everything. Every milestone. Every moment. I know I'll never get them back. But I still need to know."

So I do. Until I realize we've shifted closer on the couch and the hard line of his thigh is pressing against mine. It's distracting as hell.

Chapter 7
RAIDON

ROSA IS STARING AT me instead of the photo album. I place the album on the table and gaze at her. Her light brown eyes are dark with need. My cock hardens.

"Will you make love to me, Raidon?"

She's the most beautiful woman I've ever seen.

"Come here." I stand and hold my hand out to her, my heart a drum in my chest.

She looks up at me through her lashes, her hand trembling slightly as she slides it into mine.

I tug her to her feet, pulling her tight against my chest. She gasps, her body molding to mine like it was made just for me.

"Raidon."

I swallow her whisper, unable to resist the temptation of her mouth for another second. She opens for me immediately, her tongue tangling with mine in a slick, heated dance that has my blood roaring south.

I gentle my hands over her curves, re-learning her body. Her hips are wider, her breasts fuller. She's still the most perfect thing I've ever seen.

I break the kiss, panting against her lips. "Bedroom," I rasp, walking her backwards toward the stairs. "I want to do this right, sweetheart. Wanna make it so good for you."

She flushes, her eyes darkening farther. "The first time was pretty amazing."

I grin, my hands flexing on her hips. "Oh, it was fucking amazing, alright. But I've had twelve years to imagine all the dirty, delicious things I want to do to this body."

She shivers, her nails biting into my biceps. "Is that so?"

"Mmhmm." I capture her lips again, my tongue sweeping into her mouth in blatant imitation of what I plan to do with another part of my anatomy very soon. "You have no idea how many nights I spent with your name on my lips and my hand on my cock, Rosebud. Thinking about your tight little pussy. The way you screamed for me when I buried myself in your sweet heat."

I punctuate my words by sliding my hands down to cup her ass, grinding her against the aching bulge behind my zipper. She gasps, her head falling back. I take advantage, nuzzling the sensitive skin of her neck with lips and teeth.

"Raidon!"

I chuckle darkly, licking over the red mark I've sucked into her golden skin. "That's it, baby. Let me hear you. Fuck, I've missed the way you say my name. Like it's a prayer and a curse all at once."

We stumble up the stairs in a tangle of limbs and desperate kisses, shedding clothes as we go. By the time we hit the bed, we're both naked and panting.

I take a moment to just drink her in, my eyes feasting on acres of smooth caramel skin and dangerous curves. "Goddamn, Rosa. You're a fucking vision. I could spend hours between these thighs, my face buried deep in this pretty pussy."

She blushes, her hands fluttering over her stomach. "You can't just say things like that!"

"Why not?" I catch her wrists, pinning them gently above her head as I settle into the cradle of her hips. We both groan as my cock nestles against the slick heat of her slit. "It's the truth. I'm going to lick this sweet cunt until you're sobbing for my cock, baby. Gonna tongue fuck your clit while you scream my name."

"Oh my god." Her hips buck up involuntarily, her lower lips parting around the head of my dick like they're trying to suck me inside. "Stop talking and put your mouth on me already!"

I laugh, nipping at her jaw. "So bossy. I fucking love it."

Then I make good on my promise, kissing and licking my way down her squirming body until my shoulders push her thighs wide. She's glistening, practically dripping with need. The scent of her desire is the headiest perfume and I take a moment just to breathe her in.

"Rai, please." She's panting, her fingers fisting in my hair. I press a kiss to the inside of her knee, then the silky skin of her inner thigh.

"I got you, sweetheart. I'll give you what you need."

And then I put my mouth on her and the world narrows. She cries out, her back bowing off the bed as I lave the flat of my tongue over her weeping slit. I work her clit with merciless flicks and sucks, two fingers pumping steadily into the clenching vice of her channel.

"Oh fuck, Raidon! Don't stop, please don't stop!"

Not a chance in hell. I double my efforts, curling my fingers to massage the spongy spot behind her pubic bone as I circle and nibble her swollen clit. Her thighs squeeze my head like a vice, her nails raking over my scalp.

I can tell she's close by the way she's clamping down on my fingers, her whole body starting to quake. I latch onto her clit and suckle hard, fluttering my tongue against the sensitive bundle of nerves.

"Let go, baby. Come on my tongue. Wanna taste you falling apart for me."

That's all it takes. She shatters with a ragged scream, her release flooding my mouth and chin. I work her through it, lapping up every last drop of her nectar like a starving man at a feast.

She collapses back onto the bed, boneless and gasping. I crawl up her body, my lips and goatee glistening with her juices.

"You're fucking delicious." I lick my lips with relish. "I could feast on that pussy for hours and never get my fill."

She whimpers, pulling me down into a searing kiss. I know she can taste herself on my tongue and it only revs me higher.

"I need you inside me," she pants when we finally break apart for air. "Please, Raidon."

"I got you, sweetheart. Gonna fill this greedy little cunt so full."

I notch the blunt head of my cock against her entrance, the both of us shuddering at the contact.

"You're so tight. So wet and ready for me." I lean down, my lips brushing the shell of her ear. "Tell me, Rosa. Tell me who this pussy belongs to."

She shivers, her nails digging into the flexing muscles of my back. "You." Her eyes are glazed and heavy-lidded. "It's yours, Rai. I'm yours."

I thrust into her in one powerful surge, seating myself to the hilt in her slick heat. We both cry out at the intensity, the raw ecstasy of our joining.

"Damn right you're mine," I growl, pulling out slowly only to slam back in even harder. "This cunt was made for my cock, baby. No one else will ever touch you like this. Fill you this good."

She moans, her head thrashing on the pillow as I set a deep, driving rhythm. The obscene slap of skin on skin and our mingled cries of pleasure fill the room, spurring me on to fuck her harder, faster.

"I love you," I breathe against her mouth, my rhythm growing erratic as I feel my balls tightening in impending release. "I've loved you since that first smile you gave me over the counter. You were like sunshine after a lifetime of darkness, baby. The only pure, perfect thing in my fucked up world."

She cries out, her pussy clamping down on me like a silken fist. "I love you too," she sobs, her nails scoring down my back. "I never stopped. Even when I hated you, I loved you."

Her words undo me, the last fraying threads of my control snapping. I roar my release, my cock pulsing rope after rope of hot seed into her greedily milking cunt.

I don't know how long it's been, when I finally come back to myself, my body still blanketing hers as we gasp into each other's mouths. I'm softening inside her, our combined releases trickling out to dampen the sheets.

I feel like I finally found the missing piece of my soul.

Carefully, I pull out and roll to the side, taking her with me. She curls into my chest, one leg thrown over my hip. I wrap my arms around her, anchoring her to me.

"You're amazing," I murmur into her hair, still slightly stunned that this is real.

Rosa's fingertip traces over the letters with something like awe. "You really got my name tattooed on you?"

"Of course I did. I've been yours since the moment I laid eyes on you.

Tears swim in her eyes, her kiss-swollen lips parting on a shuddering inhale. I capture them with my own, kissing her with all the pent-up love and longing of the past decade.

When we come up for air, she nuzzles into my neck.

"I'm going to get two more, you know," I say after a long moment, my voice rough with emotion.

"Two more what?" She's already halfway to sleep, utterly spent from our lovemaking.

"Tattoos." I press a kiss to her temple, breathing in the scent of her hair. "One for each of our girls. Tamara and Tatiana. I want their names on my skin, same as their mama's."

Rosa lifts her head. "Really?"

"Really." I thumb away the stray tear that escapes down her cheek. "They're a part of me, just like you. The best parts. I want the world to know it."

She kisses me then, soft and sweet and so full of emotion it makes my chest ache. "I love you," she breathes against my lips. "We love you. The girls are going to adore you, Rai. You'll see."

God, I hope she's right. I know I have a long road ahead of me, proving myself to Rosa and our daughters, as well as her father. But I'm up for it.

I hold her close, letting the steady thrum of her heartbeat lull me into sleep.

Epilogue

ROSA

One Year later

I LEAN BACK AGAINST the pillows, totally exhausted. But it's the kind that comes from a job well done.

A chuckle from across the room snags my attention and I look up to see my husband sitting on the small sofa, our daughters perch on either side of him.

"Make sure you support his head, Tati," Raidon murmurs, helping our eldest adjust her hold on her new brother. "There you go. You're a natural."

Tatiana beams up at him, her smile so like his it makes my breath catch. Beside her, Tamara is cooing softly to the baby she's cradling, a look of absolute wonder on her face.

"They're so small," she marvels, stroking a gentle finger down a downy cheek. "Were we this little when we were born, Mama?"

"Yes," I answer.

Raidon glances at me and I can feel him checking out if I'm okay. My heart flips behind my ribs, just like it always does when faced with love in his gaze.

We've come so far as a family.

Tatiana and Tamara were wary of Raidon at first, suspicious of this stranger who had suddenly appeared and laid claim to the role of their father.

I couldn't really blame them. He'd been an abstract concept for so long, this shadowy figure who had broken my heart and disappeared into the ether. And now here he was, large as life and twice as overwhelming, trying to carve out a place for himself in our well-ordered world.

But Raidon was a steady, showing up day after day with unwavering consistency. He helped with homework and drove the girls to softball practice. He took them for rides on his motorcycle and taught them how to change a tire.

Slowly but surely, he wormed his way into their hearts.

It still sometimes catches me off guard, the depth of Raidon's love for us. For a man so gruff, he has an astounding capacity for quiet acts of devotion.

He wakes up early to pack the girls' lunches, pores over Tamara's English homework, his brow furrowed in concentration as he tries to make sense of dangling participles and split infinitives.

He even won over my father, bonding over Sunday fishing trips. He understood that I couldn't leave my father and moved in without hesitation, claiming his place in our home and our family with a resolute certainty that still sometimes steals my breath.

The girls took to their aunt Storm straight away, though, which pleased but also made Raidon jealous.

A large, warm hand on my shoulder jars me out of my reverie. I blink up at Raidon.

"You doing okay, mama?" His thumb traces over the line of my cheekbone. "You need anything?"

I lean into his touch, my eyes fluttering closed as a wave of pure contentment washes over me. This. This is everything I need. Everything I've ever wanted.

"I'm perfect," I whisper, turning my head to press a kiss to his palm.

He grins, bending to feather his lips over mine. "That you are, Rosebud. Goddamn perfect."

I hear our daughters giggling and making exaggerated gagging noises at our blatant display of affection and it only makes me smile harder against Raidon's mouth.

Later, there will be diapers to change and feedings to coordinate. Family and friends to notify and a home to baby proof. A whole new chapter of our lives to navigate as a family of six.

But right now, in this perfect bubble of a moment, I have everything I need. My daughters, healthy and happy. My sons, small and new and full of promise.

And Raidon. My once-lost love.

IRIS WEST

We've been through so much. There will be more hurdles to come, but we'll face them as a family.

SINGLE MOM AND THE NEIGHBOR

BLOSSOM FORD MOMS BOOK 4

IRIS WEST

Chapter 1
SCARLETT

THE GRIN ON CLEM'S face as we exit the hospital has me smiling too, a weight lifting off my chest. After a year of uncertainty, Clem's finally getting a clean bill of health. Her leukemia is in full remission after the bone marrow transplant. It was a long, difficult wait to find a match on the donor list, but our prayers were finally answered. The doctor just told us her monthly checkups can be stretched to every three months now.

"Mom, go see everyone in the ER while we're here," Clem suggests as we walk through the parking lot. "I know you miss them."

I ruffle her hair. "I'll see them soon enough, I only have a few days of leave left."

Clem rolls her eyes. "Mom, I'm thirteen. I can handle going to school on my own. You don't need to take me."

We playfully argue back and forth about whether she's too old to be walked to school when I nearly collide with another woman in the parking lot. "Oh, I'm so sorry."

IRIS WEST

I stop short when I realize it's Isabella Thomas from the Blossom Ford Wish Foundation, and her new husband, Riordan O'Connor. The tall, burly ex-soldier gives a solemn nod as Clem snaps to attention and executes a perfect salute. "Colonel O'Connor, sir!"

"At ease, cadet," he says with a wink.

Isabella and I exchange a smile. Ever since Riordan showed up at the hospital to grant Clem's wish of meeting him last year, she's idolized the retired para-rescue jumper. And I'll forever be grateful to Isabella, who worked for the hospital's Gift Foundation, for arranging it, especially since at the time we didn't know if Clem would make it.

I swallow hard, pushing away the dark thought. Clem is healthy and has re-started school. She'll be a cadet soon, which she's wanted to be since she decided to be a soldier like her dad, when she was only six. That's what matters.

After exchanging pleasantries with Isabella and Riordan, I hustle Clem into the car. "Alright, let's get you to school, miss independent."

"Mom," she groans, but there's a smile on her face.

After dropping her off, I pull up in front of our house, my mind preoccupied with the long to-do list waiting for me. Trash, groceries, laundry; as a single mom of three kids, the chores never end.

Lost in thought, I barely register movement next door as I fumble for my keys at the front gate. Then I glance over and see an unfamiliar man walking up to the neighboring house. It was sold months ago and has been undergoing extensive renovations, judging by the noise and the large quantities of construction materials that went into the house.

"Excuse me, are you the new neighbor?"

He pivots to face me, and all the air whooshes out of my lungs. Nobody should be allowed to look like that. Tousled jet-black hair, almond-shaped brown eyes, high cheekbones, full lips, and a strong jaw covered in stubble. And that body - broad shoulders straining against his t-shirt, lean hips, muscular thighs - I snap my gaping mouth shut, my face burning. Get it together, Scarlett!

"Yes, I just moved in," he confirms, a slight accent coloring his deep, rumbly voice. "I'm Jae Howard."

"Scarlett. Scarlett Bryant," I manage, grasping his extended hand. An electric tingle zips up my arm at the contact of his strong, slightly calloused palm against mine. "Welcome to the neighborhood."

"Thank you."

His lips curve into a soft smile, but there's heat in his eyes as they roam over me. The appreciation in his gaze sends a shiver down my spine, my nipples pebbling against my bra. Desperately needing to escape, I search for a polite exit.

"I won't keep you. I'm sure you have a lot of unpacking to do."

"It's no trouble." He takes a half-step closer, his woodsy, masculine scent enveloping me. "I'm happy to take a break to get to know my new neighbor."

"I'd better get inside. I've got mom stuff to do. Nice to meet you."

Releasing his hand, I whirl and scurry through the gate. Fumbling my keys, I finally open the door and slip inside. I lean back against it, massage my galloping heart, trying to calm my racing pulse.

I touch my hot cheek and draw a ragged breath. I haven't reacted like that to a man since Keith. Grief ripples through me, but it's not the tidal wave it used to be. Keith has been gone for six years now. Sometimes the fact that I'm living a life he'll never get to see feels like a betrayal. When he died, it was like all the light went out of the world. I didn't know how I would possibly go on without him.

But I did. For Clem, Tyler, Miles, and myself. Joy found its way back into my life. I've moved on with my life in so many ways since losing Keith. Finally bought the house we always dreamed about, even though he never got to see it. Rebuilt a life for the kids and I. His photo on the mantle doesn't make me dissolve into tears anymore.

But move on romantically? I'm not sure I'm ready for that, no matter how Jae's scorching gaze and dimpled smile make my stomach flutter.

Besides, he must be at least five years younger than my thirty-seven. He deserves a woman who can give him a fresh start, a family of his own. Not a widow with three children and stretch marks.

I'll just have to avoid him, that's all. I'm sure this attraction will fade with time. My life is full and happy as it is with the kids, my friends and the nursing career I love. I don't need the complication of a fling with the sexy neighbor, no matter how tempting he might be.

I push off the door and head to the kitchen to start lunch, my mind determinedly not lingering on soulful almond eyes and broad shoulders. I have a family to take care of and a life to live.

And no room in my careful plans for Jae Howard.

Chapter 2

JAE

I JOLT AWAKE, MY hand wrapped around my throbbing cock as it pulses in my grip, ropes of cum splattering my stomach. The vivid dream of Scarlett on her knees, those lush lips wrapped around me as she swallows every drop, fades into disappointing reality.

"Fuck," I mutter, throwing an arm over my eyes.

This is bad. Really bad. I shouldn't be fantasizing about her like this. When I met Scarlett yesterday, I clearly saw the wedding band on her finger, the bicycles scattered in the yard that could only belong to kids. She's married, a mother. Firmly off limits.

It's the one line I swore I would never cross. I don't mess with married women, period. Especially not ones with kids. After growing up in that orphanage, never knowing what it was like to have a stable family until the Howards adopted me, I could never be the one to break up a home. It goes against everything I believe in.

But damn, I can't get Scarlett out of my head. The way her cheeks flushed when our hands touched. That full bottom lip just begging to be kissed. And her eyes, warm chocolate brown with flecks of gold, gleaming with intelligence and humor even as they widened with surprise at the obvious chemistry crackling between us.

I barely slept last night, tossing and turning as I tried to banish the fantasies running through my head. I don't know how many times I imagined easing that dark silky hair out of its ponytail and running my fingers through it. Wondered if her skin was as soft as it looked. I finally gave up and went to the two rooms I had knocked together to function as my studio, thinking I could lose myself in work.

Hours later, I looked down and realized I'd sculpted Scarlett's face from memory, those stunning features and graceful curves perfectly replicated in clay. Disgusted with myself, I'd draped a cloth over the sculpture and gone out for a ride on my bike, hoping the cold morning air would clear my head. I stayed out for hours, finally stumbling back home and into bed around ten, praying I'd be too exhausted to dream. Even that was a futile hope.

Scrubbing a hand over my face, I roll out of bed and head for the shower. It's been a long time since a woman got under my skin like this. Okay, it's been a long time since I've had sex, period. Still, my reaction to Scarlett is unlike anything I've felt before. That instant zap of electricity at the lightest brush of our fingers. The way I wanted to back her up against the side of the house and taste her right there; neighbors be damned.

I crank the water to cold, hissing as the chilly spray pounds my overheated skin. When I'm clean, I shut off the water and step out, not bothering with a towel as I stalk back into the bedroom. After tossing the soiled sheets in the hamper, I pull on a pair of old jeans and a faded t-shirt.

I head outside, pick up the mail and on my way back up the front yard, spot an eleven, maybe twelve-year-old boy, scuffing his sneakers against the side of Scarlett's house as he scowls at the ground. My brow furrows at his downcast expression and the vibrant shiner darkening his left eye.

"Hey buddy. Everything okay?" I ask.

He startles at my voice, anxious gaze flying up to meet mine. "Who're you?"

"I'm Jae Howard. Just moved in next door." I nod towards my house. "I met your mom yesterday. Scarlett, right?"

The kid seems to relax slightly. "I'm Tyler."

"Nice to meet you, Tyler." I glance towards Scarlett's quiet house. "Your mom not in?"

He shakes his head.

Making a split-second decision, I jerk my chin towards my house. "I have a punching bag set up out back."

Tyler's eyes widen, guarded interest flickering across his face. He glances at his house, then back at me. Finally, he gives a jerky nod, strides out of his front yard and enters mine. He doesn't say a word as I lead him through the house and out into the backyard, to the punching bag hanging from the old tree.

I wander over to my outdoor workbench and pick up the half-formed clay I was sketching yesterday. I've been working on sculpting a pair of lovebirds nestled together on a branch, limbs entwined and beaks touching in an intimate gesture. A commission piece for an anniversary present. I guide the clay into smooth lines and delicate feathers. The steady rhythm of Tyler's punches fades into the background as I lose myself in the work, everything else falling away.

"What are you making?"

Tyler's question jolts me out of my creative haze. I blink, looking up to find him standing a few feet away, chest heaving and hair sweat-soaked, but eyes clearer than before.

"They're lovebirds," I explain, tilting the sculpture so he can see better. "I'm a sculptor."

"They're really good!"

I grab a spare hunk of clay, I cut off a piece and hold it out to him. "Want to try? Just play around with it, see what shapes and textures you can create."

Tyler takes the clay with careful fingers and digs into the pliable surface with his thumbs. We work in easy silence for a few minutes, until I think he might be ready to talk.

"Want to talk about the shiner?"

Tyler freezes, shoulders hunching up around his ears again. His fingers clench around the clay. I wait. Pushing will only make him clam up tighter.

"It's stupid."

"I doubt that."

He shrugs, picking at the clay. "A boy at school was talking crap about my sister. She's been out for almost two years because she was sick. Had to get held back and now she's in my grade."

Protective anger surges in my gut on this family's behalf.

"He said Clem probably wouldn't even graduate. That chemo made her a retard, so she should just drop out now and quit wasting everyone's time."

"Tyler, I'm sorry! What a mean thing to say."

"I hit him."

"You stood up for your sister. That's never wrong."

"Even if it got me into trouble?"

"Even then, but you have to accept the consequences, like a man, whatever they are."

"Is that what you did?"

"Yes. I hated it when the other kids called me names because I was different. But, later, I realized they wanted to provoke me so I'd get in trouble."

"Like me," Tyler mutters.

"Yeah. So, I stopped letting them win by ignoring them."

"That's hard."

"I know. Still, I wasn't making my parents sad and soon, the kids got bored and stopped messing with me."

He sighs, and is quiet for a while, as if thinking about what I said.

"It's just me, my little brother, sister and mom. My dad passed away while defending our country."

"Tyler, I'm so sorry."

A quick, jerky headshake. "It was a long time ago."

The grief thickening his words tells me he still misses his dad. My heart hurts for him and Scarlett. For all of them. I think about what it must have been like for her, losing her husband and having to raise three young kids on her own.

"Your dad would be damn proud of you looking out for your sister."

Tears swim in his eyes but don't fall, his chin trembling with the effort of holding them back. "I should head home. Mom must be back."

"Okay. But you ever need to talk, blow off steam, or explore with clay, come on over, anytime."

Tyler smiles and gazes at the clay he played with, eagerness gleaming in his eyes.

Scarlett isn't married. She's raising three children alone, which makes her strong and sexy on top of being the most beautiful woman I've ever met. I want her. Want to know her inside and out and cherish her.

Chapter 3
SCARLETT

THE SOUND OF VOICES outside the front door has me hastily tying my hair up in a ponytail as I hurry out of the bathroom. Ty should have been home by now and after the call I received from school, I'm worried he might have gotten into trouble outside school.

I tug the door open, only to stop short at the sight of my son standing next to... Jae?

"Hey, Mom." Tyler shifts from foot to foot, a guilty flush staining his cheeks. My eyes widen at the vivid purple bruise darkening his left eye.

Maternal instinct kicks into high gear as I reach for him, gently turning his face to examine the contusion. He squirms out of my grasp, ducking his head.

"I'm fine, Mom."

I glance at Jae, an unspoken question in my gaze. His expression softens as he meets my eyes, something warm and reassuring in their toffee depths. "He's okay, Scarlett. We were just hanging out."

Clem comes up beside me, followed by Miles, my eight-year-old. They both look up at our unexpected guest, curiosity bright on their faces.

"Who's that?" Miles asks.

"This is Mr. Howard. He's our new next-door neighbor. He's good with his hands, he was showing me how to sculpt." Tyler says.

"Hi Mr. Howard! I'm Miles. I like your motorcycle!"

Jae chuckles, the rich sound sending tingles cascading down my spine. "Maybe I can take you for a ride sometime, if your mom says it's okay."

I bite the inside of my cheek hard, desperately trying to get a grip on my rioting hormones. What is it about this man that affects me so strongly?

"My rocket ship nightlight is broken. Mom tried to fix it, but it's still broken. Please, can you help fix it?"

"Miles, I'm sure Mr. Howard has better things to do than -"

"I don't mind," Jae interrupts. "I'd be happy to look. Let me just grab my toolbox from the house."

With a wink at Miles, he strides down the steps and across the yard, that predatory grace making my mouth go dry. Forcing my gaze away, I usher the kids back inside and shut the door.

I turn to Tyler. "School called. They said you got into a fight?"

He scuffs a toe against the welcome mat, shoulders hunching.

"I know you won't hit another child without a reason, Ty."

"He said something mean about another kid."

"It was about me, wasn't it? It's okay, you can tell us," Clem says.

"Tyler?" I keep my voice gentle. "You want to tell me what that boy said about Clem?"

"He said chemo messed her mind up, that she's wasting everyone's time coming back to school. I couldn't let him talk about Clem like that, Mom."

Clem makes a wounded noise. I wrap an arm around her shoulders and pull her close. "I'm so sorry, baby. People can be cruel when they're scared of what they don't understand."

"I don't care what he thinks," she says, though the wobble in her voice gives away the lie. "I just don't want Ty getting in trouble because of me. I'm his older sister. I should protect him, not the other way round."

"You let me handle the school stuff." I drop a kiss on her head. "And Ty, I am so proud of you for sticking up for Clem. You have such a good heart. We just need to work on finding better ways to channel that protectiveness, okay?"

"I'll handle the consequences. Mr. Howard gave me some good advice, in case it happens again. I'll just ignore him."

I blink. In all the times we've had this conversation, this has to be the first time Tyler hasn't grumbled about the unfairness of getting punished for retaliating when someone else picked on him first.

"Why don't you all grab a snack and start your homework? I need to talk to Mr. Howard for a minute when he comes."

As the kids disperse into the house, I take a deep breath. I'm grateful that Jae took the time to speak to Ty and could explain things in a way the boy clearly understood. But I'm not used to having anyone outside of my family help.

A knock sounds, and I jerk out of my thoughts to find Jae standing on the other side of the screen door, carrying a toolbox.

"Thank you for talking to Tyler. And thanks for this, you don't have to do it."

"I want to. It was good to see Tyler fell a little better." There's a world of meaning layered under those three small words, an unspoken 'let me help' that simultaneously thrills and terrifies me.

I push open the door and lead him inside. Miles barrels out of the kitchen, chocolate smeared at the corners of his mouth. "Mr. Howard, you're back!"

"'Course I am. Why don't you show me your rocket ship nightlight?"

Miles leads Jae upstairs, Tyler hovering close behind.

I trail after them, a prickle of awareness dancing along my skin at the knowledge that Jae is in my house.

I hover in the doorway to Miles' bedroom, watching as Jae efficiently dismantles the nightlight, long clever fingers making quick work of the tiny screws. Tyler passes him tools while Miles perches on the bed and peppers him with questions about his motorcycle.

And of course, my traitorous body notices the way Jae's forearms flex as he works, the shift of muscle under his skin, the furrow of concentration between his brows. A trickle of sweat between my breasts has me shifting restlessly, the low-level arousal that's been simmering since our charged first meeting yesterday kicking up a notch.

I hoped this awareness for Jae would disappear after a few hours of sleep. Instead, I tossed and turned in bed, unable to stop thinking about what being in his arms would feel like. It got so bad, the needy ache between my thighs so insistent, I finally caved and touched myself for the first time in six years.

Watching the easy way he jokes with the kids, the open affection on his face, makes me wonder how it would feel to be his woman.

Chapter 4
JAE

"DONE," I SAY AFTER testing the nightlight twice. "Any problems, give me a shout, okay?"

"Thanks, Mr. Howard!" Tyler's bright smile is a far cry from the brooding, hurt boy I met earlier. Satisfaction settles warm and heavy in my chest at having played even a small role in that transformation.

"Yeah, thanks! You're the best!" Miles says, his green eyes glowing.

Chuckling, I ruffle his hair.

We head downstairs, and I have to keep my eager pace in check, because Scarlett is there.

She appears in the hallway, and I'm amazed by how gorgeous she is. That fall of midnight hair, the soft femininity of her curves, makes it hard to wrench my gaze from her.

Tyler's sister sticks out a hand for me to shake. "I'm Clementine, but everyone calls me Clem. Thanks for fixing Miles' nightlight."

"It's nice to meet you, Clem."

From what Tyler said, she's about thirteen, but her eyes show maturity beyond her years.

"Mom," Clem says, "You could show Mr. Howard around town. He's been kind to us."

"Yeah, Mom, like you did with Mr. Kennedy," Miles adds.

One corner of Scarlett's mouth ticks up even as she shakes her head. "Baby, Mr. Kennedy was in his seventies. I'm sure Mr. Howard will not need my help."

Miles scrunches his nose.

"But Mom, you said we should help our neighbors. You even helped Miss. Crystal and she's lots younger than you."

"That's right," Tyler says.

"Yes, Mom," Clem adds, a sly twinkle in her eye that tells me she's not oblivious to the tension snapping between her mom and I. "You love showing off Blossom Ford. And this weekend is perfect - we'll be at Grandma and Grandpa's, and I bet Auntie Rosa, Auntie Sienna, and Auntie Destiny will be too busy with their new boyfriends to hang out with you."

Scarlett shoots her daughter a look, but I can see her wavering.

"I'd really appreciate it." When she glances at me, I hold her gaze. "I'm hoping to make Blossom Ford my home, but it's a little daunting, moving to a new place alone. Especially since this is such a small town. I'd feel so much better about it if I had a friend to show me around." I paste on my most charming smile.

"If you're sure," Scarlett says.

"I am," I say firmly.

I'm sure that I want to spend every spare minute drinking her in. The instant, searing attraction between us is something rare and precious. I just know that Scarlett is everything I've ever wanted. I need to do whatever it takes to win not just her breathtaking body, but her guarded heart.

She takes a shaky breath, gaze searching mine. I let her look, let her see the open want, the raw honesty. After a beat, she nods, a jerky dip of her chin that has elation zipping through me. "Okay. I'll pick you up on Friday afternoon, if that works?"

"Perfect," I rasp, so much unspoken promise layered into that single word.

She walks me to the front door. "Thank you for being so wonderful with the kids."

Pride and protectiveness surge in my chest, fierce and hot. I'm already half in love with her children. "You've got great kids. I enjoy spending time with them."

"Still." She takes a deep breath. "When Tyler came home today, with that black eye, I was worried about how to make him understand violence isn't always the best approach to take. You helped him get that. It means everything to me, Jae."

My name on her lips, husky with emotion, lights me up from the inside. I take a shaky breath of my own, fighting the need to reach for her. To yank her into my arms and show her one way I want to be there for her.

"I'm next door. Come get me if you need any help."

I take a reluctant step back, needing to put some distance between us before I do something crazy, like kiss her senseless against the doorjamb.

When the door shuts, I force myself back to my place. This weekend is a precious gift - uninterrupted time with Scarlett, a chance to show her how good we could be together. To peel back the layers and find the passionate woman I know is hiding under that polite smile and practical ponytail.

Chapter 5
SCARLETT

I STARE AT MY reflection in the bathroom mirror, hardly recognizing the woman looking back at me. My hair is down, a cascade of dark waves over my shoulders instead of my usual sensible ponytail. A swipe of mascara and a dab of tinted lip balm are the only concessions I've made to makeup, but combined with the flush of anticipation heating my cheeks, I look like a woman going out to meet her boyfriend.

Shaking my head at my foolishness, I smooth my hands down the front of my usual tunic dress and leggings, taking comfort in the familiar fabrics. When I'd finally worked up the nerve to text Jae about showing him around town this afternoon, a thrill had zipped through me at his immediate, enthusiastic response. Suddenly, the idea of putting actual effort into my appearance, into being more than just Mom, seemed far too tempting.

I'd even started mentally sorting through my closet for date-worthy outfits before reality crashed in and I reminded myself this wasn't a date. Just a friendly gesture for a new neighbor, one I'd extend to anyone.

A honk from the driveway startles me into action. My stomach swoops as I hurry out the door, scanning Jae's dark head near his motorcycle. When I spot him leaning against the mailbox instead, arms crossed over his broad chest and a smile playing about his lips, my steps falter.

He's devastating. The late afternoon sun burnishes his olive skin and brings out the lighter streaks in his rumpled hair. A gray henley stretches across his shoulders, the fabric molding to every perfect ridge of muscle.

"Hey." His husky greeting snaps me out of my ogling. Horrified heat crawls up my neck as I realize I'm just standing here, staring at him like a tongue-tied teenager.

"You ready to see the beautiful town of Blossom Ford?"

His smile widens, showing a flash of even white teeth. "I'm all yours."

A shiver rolls through me at the silken promise in those words. Averting my gaze, I fumble my keys out of my purse and unlock the car.

The minute we're both settled in our seats, the air seems to thicken. Every breath draws Jae's scent into my lungs, an intoxicating mix of pine, musk, and man. As I turn the key in the ignition, the rumble of the engine vibrates through me, adding to the low-level thrum of arousal his nearness always seems to incite.

Swallowing hard, I check my mirrors and carefully pull away from the curb, all too aware of Jae's eyes on my profile and those long, lean thighs inches from my own.

This was a terrible idea.

"So where to first?"

I clear my throat. "I figured we could start at the top of Maine Street, hit the essential spots. Not that there's all that much to see."

"Sounds perfect."

Out of the corner of my eye, I catch his smile. Not the knee-weakening playboy grin I've seen him use but something more intimate. As if this rambling tour of my hometown is the only place in the world he wants to be.

I shove down the tiny tendril of pleasure that takes root in my belly at the thought. I'm reading way too much into a simple quirk of lips.

"Well, here we have Rosa's Treats, home to the most sinful pies this side of the Mississippi. Get here early on weekends if you want any chance of snagging a buttermilk pie before they sell out."

"You a big pie fan?"

"Who isn't?" The laugh trips off my tongue, easy and unforced. "And if you want to bribe the kids into mowing your lawn, a box of Rosa's Treats' buttermilk pies is the currency of choice."

Jae chuckles.

I point out all the places I think he needs to know, like the grocery store, a bank, hospital and pub.

Through it all, Jae pays rapt attention. He asks questions about growing up in Blossom Ford, about the kids' favorite activities, and about my work at the hospital. Draws out funny anecdotes and long-buried memories with an ease that startles me. Makes me wonder how I'm already confiding in him things I've never shared with anyone.

"Okay, last stop - Jackson's Diner," I announce as I pull up in front of the low-slung building. "Best grilled cheese and milkshakes for miles. Not exactly fine dining, but it's the social hub around here."

"No judgment here. You had me at grilled cheese." He glances towards the diner, then back at me, a hint of mischief playing about his sinful mouth. "Split a shake with me?"

The automatic denial dies on my tongue as I take in his playful expression. Suddenly, the thought of walking into Jackson's with Jae at my side feels dangerous and reckless, yet unbelievably tempting.

But the risk of fueling the town's gossip mill is too high. I shake my head reluctantly. "Better not. If we go in there together, people will assume we're dating."

Jae's eyes flash with something fierce and hungry. "Would that be so bad?"

My breath catches at the implication, heat creeping up my neck. Needing air, I abruptly head towards Blossom Ford Point, where I can be out in the open. The silence in the car is charged, heavy with words unspoken.

I park near the riverside and climb out, desperate to escape the confines of the car. Jae follows wordlessly as I make my way down to the water's edge, the setting sun painting the sky in streaks of orange and pink.

We stand there, side by side, watching the light dance across the rippling surface. The simple beauty of it soothes my racing heart.

After a while, I feel the weight of his gaze on my profile. Slowly, I turn to face him, and the breath leaves my lungs in a rush.

His eyes are molten, searing me with the intensity of his desire. In their brown depths, I glimpse my reflection - lips parted, cheeks flushed, an answering hunger in my expression that rocks me to my core.

Jae steps closer, a large, warm hand coming up to cup my cheek. I tremble at the contact, my eyes fluttering shut as he leans in, his breath a whisper across my lips.

And then he's kissing me, a slow, drugging slide of his mouth over mine that has me melting into him. I wind my arms around his neck, pressing closer, losing myself in the delicious heat of him.

When he finally pulls back, we're both breathing hard, our foreheads touching.

"I want to date you, Scarlett." Jae's voice is rough, scraped raw with want. "I want to take you out, spoil you, make you feel as special as you are."

My heart is a drum in my chest. "Jae, I can't do casual relationships. I have the kids to think about. Also, you're so much younger than me."

"I'm thirty-one, Scarlett. Old enough to know what I want." He strokes a thumb across my cheekbone, his touch impossibly gentle. "And what I want is you. You and the kids. I'm in this for life, if you'll have me."

Tears burn the backs of my eyes at the raw sincerity in his words. I want so badly to believe him, to trust that I could be enough for this amazing man.

"What exactly are you saying, Jae?" I whisper.

He cups my face in his larger, rough hands, his gaze branding me with its intensity. "I'm saying I want forever with you, Scarlett. I've never felt like this about anyone before. You're the woman I want to spend my life with, to build a family with. And I'll do whatever it takes to prove that to you."

Chapter 6
SCARLETT

I STARE UNSEEINGLY AT the glass of wine in my hand, my friends' chatter and laughter of fading into background noise as my mind drifts, yet again, to Jae.

I've been avoiding him all day, the memory of last night's charged kiss at the river's edge playing on a loop in my head. The way he'd looked at me, desire and adoration burning in those almond eyes, the feather-soft brush of his lips against mine, a promise and a plea all in one.

I wanted so badly to say yes when he asked to date me, but the sheer want pulsing through my veins clashed against my habit of always putting others first. I worried about the kids, Jae missing out on starting a family and Keith. So, I stammered something about needing time to think and practically sprinted for the car.

Jae simply held out a hand for the keys and drove us home. And when he walked me to my door, his voice had been rough with restraint as he told me to take as long as I needed and he'd be waiting next door whenever I was ready to talk.

I'd managed a nod before escaping into the house, my knees weak and my core molten. I'd tossed and turned all night, reliving the heat of his kiss, the drugging slide of his tongue against mine. Imagining the rasp of his stubble on my inner thighs, the blunt edges of his fingers as he...

"Earth to Scarlett!" Sienna's laughing voice yanks me out of my indecent musings.

I take in the amused and curious faces of my three closest friends, my family, really. Destiny, Sienna, and Rosa are sprawled around my living room, wineglasses in hand and matching Cheshire Cat grins on their faces.

"What?" I ask.

"We were just discussing the delicious piece of man candy you were spotted with yesterday," Destiny says, a gleam in her honey-brown eyes. "Spill, girl. Who is he?"

I groan, taking a fortifying sip of wine. "My new neighbor: Jae Howard. He just moved in next door."

"And you're already going on romantic sunset strolls?" Rosa waggles her eyebrows suggestively.

"It wasn't a date," I protest, but even I can hear the lack of conviction in my voice. "I was just showing him around town."

"Sure." Sienna twirls a glossy curl around her finger, a knowing smirk playing about her lips. "Because platonic tours always end with steamy gazes and almost-kisses. We have eyes, honey."

I flatten a hand over my stomach, trying to calm the riot of butterflies her words incite. Helplessly, I blurt out the first thing that comes to mind. "He's six years younger than me!"

Sienna's brows shoot up. "So?"

"So, he's practically a kid!" I ignore the voice in my head that whispers how very un-childlike the flex of his muscles and the heat in his eyes had been. "And even if he wasn't, I loved Keith."

Understanding softens Destiny's expression. She reaches over to squeeze my hand, her skin warm against my chilled fingers. "Oh, honey. I know how much you loved Keith. How much losing him shattered you. But it's been six years. Do you really think he'd want you to close yourself off from love forever?"

"Some days, it feels like I'll never be ready. I'm afraid of getting attached again. Of risking the kids' hearts when they've already lost so much."

"But you are attached," Rosa points out gently. "To Jae. I've never seen you look at anyone the way you were looking at him last night. And you're a great judge of character. If you trust him, he's going to be good to your kids."

A shaky laugh escapes me, because she's not wrong. In such a short time, Jae has burrowed under my skin.

"Do you remember what you told me when Raidon came back into my life?" Rosa asks, ducking her head to catch my gaze. "You said I had a choice. To let fear rule me or to take a chance on the love that's right in front of me. Maybe it's your turn to take that chance."

The last of my resistance crumbles. Because the girls are right. This thing with Jae is powerful. The thought of letting it go because I'm too scared to reach for it? It feels like the worst kind of cowardice.

I straighten up, squaring my shoulders as determination settles over me. "Okay."

Sienna pulls me into an exuberant hug. "That's our brave, beautiful big sister! I don't know what I would have done without your help, when I arrived in Blossom Ford alone and pregnant. You deserve happiness."

I laugh against her shoulder, soaking in her love and support.

Destiny joins in the hug. "Me too, big sis."

Rosa pulls them off me, but I see the tears in her eyes. "Let's go so our bis sis can get her man."

After a final round of hugs and well wishes, I see them out, butterflies rioting in my stomach in anticipation of what I'm about to do.

I run upstairs, take off my wedding ring, and gently place it in the box on the top shelf of the closet.

Drawing a steadying breath, I go downstairs. I slip out the door and cross the yard to Jae's house before I lose my nerve.

My hand trembles as I knock on his door. Moments later, it swings open.

Jae steps back to let me in, and I brush past him.

"I'm sorry for running away last night. This is all so new and intense. I'm scared, Jae, of being left alone and risking the kids' hearts when they've already been through so much."

Tenderness softens his rugged features. He takes a careful step towards me, his hands gentle as they frame my face. "I know, baby. I will never intentionally hurt you or the kids."

"I want to try."

He rests his forehead against mine. "We'll figure this out together."

The conviction in his voice, the steadfast promise in his gaze, is like a balm on all my wounded places.

I wind my arms around his neck, press our bodies flush so that sparks skitter down my spine.

Jae makes a rough sound deep in his chest, his grip tightening on my hips

When he ducks to capture my lips with his, the last of my reservations melt away.

Chapter 7

JAE

THE MOMENT SCARLETT ADMITS she'll give this thing between us a chance, a dam break inside me. The pent-up longing, and the bone-deep certainty that she's the one I've been waiting for my whole life crashes over me in a wave of so fierce, it steals my breath.

I capture her mouth in a kiss that's pure heat and hunger. Her fingers tangle in my hair as she opens to the demanding sweep of my tongue. I groan into the slick cavern of her mouth.

We stumble backwards, knocking into furniture as we tug at clothes with increasing desperation. The raw urgency, the primal need to be skin to skin, overrides any thought of making it to the bedroom. All I can focus on is getting my hands on her, learning her curves and secret places until I know them better than my name.

"Jae," she pants against my lips, my name a plea in her husky voice.

I guide her onto the couch, drinking her in as she lies sprawled beneath me. Her midnight hair is a tousled cloud against the pale cushions, her lips kiss-swollen and her eyes heavy-lidded with want. The swell of her breasts strains against her bra, and I swear I can see the hammering of her pulse in the delicate column of her throat.

She's the most beautiful thing I've ever seen.

I skim my fingertips along the lush curves of her body, marveling at the contrast of my tanned skin against her rich mocha complexion. She shivers under my touch, a soft moan escaping her as I trace the scalloped edges of her bra.

"You're perfect," I rasp, my voice scraped raw with adoration. "So fucking perfect, Scarlett. I can't believe that you're here with me."

She flushes, ducking her head as she plucks at the hem of her shirt. "I'm not... My body isn't the same as it was before I had the kids. There are stretch marks and scars and things that sag that didn't use to."

I cut her off with a hard, deep kiss, stopping that train of thought in its tracks. "I'm going to love your body," I growl against her lips. "Every single inch of it. You're the sexiest woman I've ever seen, Scarlett."

A broken sound escapes her, her nails digging into my shoulders as she arches into me. I trail open-mouthed kisses down her throat, across her collarbone, and between her breasts.

"I love that your body shows the signs of the life you've lived," I murmur, slowly peeling her shirt up to reveal the smooth skin of her belly. A faded silver line slashes across the expanse just below her navel, and I follow its path with my fingertip.

"Your cesarean scar," I breathe, pressing my lips to the puckered flesh. "The mark of your strength, your sacrifice. You brought life into this world, Scarlett. There is no greater beauty than that."

She inhales shakily, her fingers sliding into my hair to cradle my head against her. I lavish kisses across the scar, savoring the quiver of her muscles, the hitching of her breath.

"This is one of the many reasons I fell in love with you," I tell her, dropping a final, lingering kiss above the top of her jeans. "With everything that makes you, you."

Her eyes shimmer with unshed tears as I crawl back up her body to hover over her. She loops her arms around my neck, a tremulous smile playing about her kiss-reddened lips. "Only one of the reasons, huh? What are the others?"

I grin, nipping playfully at her mouth. "Your courage, for one." I dust a kiss across her cheekbone. "The way you never give up, even when life keeps knocking you down." Another to the tip of her nose. "Your fierce love for your kids, your selflessness in always putting them first." The corner of her jaw, the sensitive spot behind her ear. "Your kindness, the way you see people."

I pull back to meet her gaze, my heart in my eyes. "Every little thing that happened to you, every moment of joy and grief and hope and pain, shaped you into the incredible woman you are. The woman I'm hopelessly in love with."

A single tear slips down her cheek, and I catch it with my thumb.

She surges up to crash her mouth to mine, the kiss sweeter than anything I've ever tasted. "I'm in love with you, too," she gasps between desperate presses of lips.

Jo warms my heart. I pour every ounce into the kiss, my hands roaming greedily over her body as I peel her clothes and yank mine off.

"Please," Scarlett mewls when I finally have her bare beneath me, miles of satiny brown skin for me to explore.

"You're beautiful, baby!"

My cock is dripping from looking at her.

I palm her breasts, thumbs grazing the beaded peaks. She mewls when I take a nipple into my mouth, arching like a bow as I suck hard. I lathe the sensitive bud with my tongue, reveling in her broken cries, the dig of her fingers in my hair. I feel more pre-cum seep out of the slit of my dick and reluctantly releasing her nipple.

"I need to be inside you, Scarlett."

"Make me yours, Jae."

I insert a finger into her and groan at how wet she is. I slide in two more digits, rubbing the heel of my hand against her engorged clit.

Scarlett moans.

She's pants my name, nails scoring my back as she writhes against my hand. I pull my soaking fingers out of her pussy and my cock at her entrance, holding her gaze as I push inside in one long, smooth glide.

"Jae!"

The feel of her, hot and tight and perfect around me, drives the breath from my lungs. I have to clench my eyes shut, my arms trembling with the effort to hold still, to give her a moment to adjust. But then she rocks her hips and I'm lost.

I take her with deep, driving thrusts, swiveling my hips on every downstroke to hit a spot that makes her keen. She matches me thrust for thrust, her heels digging into my ass as she urges me harder, faster, deeper.

"Jae," she chants, her head thrashing on the cushions as I angle my thrusts to rub against her clit. "Oh god, don't stop, I'm so close, I'm going to-"

I feel her shatter in my arms, her orgasm rippling through her in great, shuddering waves. My balls draw up tight, the pressure building at the base of my spine, and I try to push the release back to give her another orgasm but the rhythmic clench of her pussy milks my own orgasm from me, and I spill into her pulsing depths with a roar, her name on my lips.

Still lodged inside her soaked channel, I gather her limp form against my chest, petting sweat-slick skin as I pepper her face with kisses. "I love you," I rasp, the words scraped raw. "You're mine now, Scarlett. My fucking always."

IRIS WEST

She nuzzles into my throat, sighing contentedly. "My always."

Epilogue

SCARLETT

Five Years later

THE FIRST THING I notice as I drift into wakefulness is the silence. No patter of little feet, no creak of floorboards, no muffled giggles. Just blessed, uninterrupted quiet.

I stretch languidly, a smile tugging at my lips. Jae must have taken the kids on their usual morning hike, letting me sleep in after the grueling week of back-to-back shifts at the hospital. Warmth blooms in my chest at his thoughtfulness, the small ways he's always looking out for me.

Suddenly, the front door bangs open, followed by a chorus of shushes and stifled laughter. They're trying so hard to be quiet, but subtlety has never been my brood's strong suit. The clatter of dishes and utensils floats up the stairs.

I'm just about to lever myself out of bed when my bedroom door cracks open. Clem pokes her head in. She puts a finger to her lips, nodding to someone behind her, and a moment later my youngest, four-year-old Yara, bursts into the room with all the grace of a baby elephant.

A laugh threatens to bubble up my throat, but I quickly smother it, schooling my features into a mask of pretend slumber. The girls creep closer on exaggerated tiptoes; the bed dipping as they clamber up beside me.

"Mama?" Yara whispers loudly, patting my cheek. "Mama, wake up!"

"Surprise!" Clem and Yara chorus, as I let my eyes flutter open. Yara flings herself at me in a full-body hug while Clem kisses my cheek.

"Well, good morning to you, too!" I gather them close. "To what do I owe this wonderful wake-up call?"

"I helped Clem set the table!" Yara proclaims proudly.

"Jae, Ty and Miles made pancakes! Come on, it's getting cold," Clem says.

I let them tug me out of bed and down the stairs, pausing to throw on one of Jae's flannel shirts. As we enter the kitchen, two tousled heads pop up from behind the counter, wide grins splitting their faces.

"Morning, Mom." Tyler is all gangly limbs and oversized feet. At sixteen, he's shot up like a beanstalk, his once cherubic features sharpening into the striking angles of manhood. Looking at him now, I can hardly reconcile this self-assured young man with the angry, grieving boy he was when Jae first came into our lives.

Miles throws his arms around my waist in a quick squeeze before bounding back to the stove. "Mom, I made the eggs!" he announces, chest puffing with pride. "Dad showed me how to get them all fluffy, and I didn't burn a single one!"

"Sounds delicious, sweetheart." I ruffle his hair, marveling at how much he's grown, too. My baby boy, already eleven.

Jae sidles up behind me as I survey the crowded table, strong arms banding around my waist. "Morning, beautiful," he murmurs, lips grazing my temple. "Sleep well?"

I hum contentedly, leaning back into his solid warmth. "Very. You didn't have to let me snooze the day away, you know."

He nips playfully at my ear. "You needed the rest."

As we settle around the table, my heart swells at the easy banter, the clinking silverware, and the carefree laughter around the table.

I still remember those early days of dating, the butterflies and hesitant hopes. Jae tucked himself seamlessly into our lives, cheering at the boys' games and helping Clem with schoolwork. He heartily joined family dinners, movie nights, and trips to the park. The kids loved the way he put them first, like any dad would. By the time he proposed three months in, I didn't hesitate. Marrying him felt as natural as breathing.

Two months later, as I stared at a positive pregnancy test, and I couldn't be happier. I wanted Jae to experience making a life and seeing it grow in my womb. We married two months later, with our kids as our flower boys and girl and Rosa, Destiny and Sienna as my maids of honor.

The kids love having three sets of grandparents – Keith's, mine and Jae's parents. Every summer break, they spend a week with each set of grandparents and Jae and I get to travel and spend some alone time.

And Ty, my heart squeezes as I watch him tinker with the delicate filigree he's been working on, clever fingers deft and sure. Jae sparked a passion for sculpting in him that's become such an integral part of who he is, the anger that once consumed him finding a positive outlet. He comes alive in Jae's studio, a mirror of the focused intensity I see so often in my husband's eyes.

After breakfast, the kids shoo us out of the kitchen, insisting they'll clean up. Jae laces his fingers with mine, tugging me towards the back porch. The sprawling yard has seen its fair share of soccer games and tea parties, the fence between our properties long since torn down.

Jae pulls me into his lap on the porch swing, arms cocooning me in contentment. "Happy anniversary, gorgeous."

I twist to loop my arms around his neck, fingers sifting through the silky strands at his nape. "Happy anniversary. Ready for an entire week, just the two of us?"

"God, yes." He dips to nibble along my jaw. "I'm going to worship this body morning, noon, and night. Relearn every curve, find new ways to make you scream."

I shiver, arousal a warm coil in my belly. "Promises, promises." The rasp of his stubble reignites the memories of our last trip to Bali, the wanton abandonment of those sun-drenched days.

He chuckles, low and dark, but sobers as he gazes down at me. My breath hitches as he tucks a stray curl behind my ear.

"Thank you," he murmurs, voice gruff with emotion. "Thank you for being mine. You and the kids complete me, Scarlett."

After learning he was abandoned at an orphanage in his native country of South Korea and how long it took him to believe his adoptive American parents loved him, I always wanted him to feel loved. "Thank you for being ours. I love you so damn much," I say.

Moisture glints in his eyes as he hauls me closer. "My always."

"My always,"

Fancy more short and steamy instalove boxsets from Iris West? Check out Curvy Brides Of Blossom Ford Books 1-4.

FREE BOOK

Would you like a free book? Sign up to my mailing list at https://dl.bookfunnel.com/t191w45ryj to receive a copy of Loving My Fake Husband, a Curvy Brides of Blossom Ford Series short story.

HELP OTHERS FIND THIS BOOK

Thank you for reading Blossom Ford Moms. If you enjoyed this book, please help others discover it by leaving a review. Many thanks,

Iris xx

ABOUT THE AUTHOR

Iris West writes short and steamy romance about alpha heroes and the women they can't help falling in love with. She loves reading all types of romance books that have a happy ending and is an avid Kdrama fan.

Follow or like her on Facebook, Bookbub, Amazon, Goodreads, Tiktok and/or Instagram.

Printed in Dunstable, United Kingdom